We make plans for life only to realize that life has plans for us. That's why we have instructions to follow. There is a manual on life. Like anything else, when we try to put something together without reading the manual and follow the instructions, it falls apart.

Marvin is a seventeen year old senior that's about to graduate from high school in a few of months. He maintains a 'B' average while playing both basketball and football. He's very sociable, blending smoothly with both students and faculty. Everybody knows you can find Marvin running or in the gym working out, and at 6'3" 230 pounds he's a monster on the field. Always worrying about his appearance, Marvin keeps his hair trimmed short and wavy and dresses neatly, often wearing a shirt and tie to school.

With high school ending for him in two months, he starts to think more about his future and wants to continue his education. College scouts are looking at him on the field and he has hopes of getting scholarships to help pay for school while he saves money from working.

With his school schedule being a half day, it allows him to work a full-time job in the evening

2

from 2p.m. to 10p.m. at a printing office. But he plans to go to college and major in Information Technology. Marvin feels he has it all figured out.

It's Friday and almost lunch time at Marvin's school, however to Marvin, it is pay day and the beginning of his weekend. Sitting in class feeling impatient while everybody else is talking, Marvin starts putting his books in his backpack while glancing at the clock on the wall. Its 11:58 am, two minutes before the bells rings and it feels like a life time to Marvin. Feeling like ten minutes had gone by, he looks at the clock again only to see one minute passed. Marvin starts shaking his head while everyone else is still chatting away. Finally the bell rings and it's lunch time but to Marvin it's the beginning of his weekend. He jumps up, throws his backpack on one shoulder while shouting to the class, "See yall later! Got to go." Marvin runs out the classroom.

Marvin is in a hurry because it's pay day and he wants to cash his check before work starts. He runs down the hall squeezing between people hoping to catch the 12:05 p.m. bus to his job with hopes of cashing his check before starting work. Slamming his locker shut, he ran to the front of the school and plows through the doors. Marvin sees the bus at the corner stop sign about to make the turn to the bus stop. He jumps over the steps and starts to speed up running while yelling to people "Hold the bus! Hold the bus!" Finally reaching the bus, he runs beside it and it pulls off. Feeling angry about missing the bus, he starts to think he won't be able to cash his check before work. He kicks a soda can and walks over to the bus schedule to find out when the next bus is coming. After finding out that the next bus wouldn't be arriving for at least forty minutes, he sits down and plays with his cell phone. Looking at the time, Marvin gave up on getting his check cashed before work.

Now he's bored with playing the same game on his phone, so he starts searching for new games. Finding nothing interesting, he starts checking out cars as they ride by. Glancing up from his phone, he sees a new pretty pearl white M3 convertible BMW that really gets his attention. His mouth dropped open and all he could say is, "Wow!" Marvin really admires this car with 22 inch chrome rims and the top down. This car took his mind off of missing the bus and his pay check.

While watching this car ride by, Marvin notices it stopped in the middle of the street and made a U-turn. Marvin watched this car coming towards him and stopped. He starts to wonder if he knows the driver, but he doesn't think so. Then the driver yells, "yo cuz! What you doing at the bus stop?"

Marvin recognizes the voice. It's his old middle school buddy Chucky.

Marvin jumps up looking both ways while running out in the street over to Chucky with his fist out, "man what's up? I didn't recognize you with a bald head and a beard, mannnnnn, is this your car?"

Chucky looks at Marvin with his eyes looking over his sunshades and smiles, "Where you going, cuz? You need a ride?" Marvin feeling excited, "yeah man, I need to go downtown." Chucky waves his hand, "come on I gotcha." Marvin runs around to the passenger side and gets in the car. He is checking out the inside, "man this car is like that." He starts touching the dash and the soft leather seat, "man who car is this? "It ain't stolen, is it?"

Chucky looks at Marvin, "cuz relax! Nah, it ain't stolen. I don't have to steal." "I'm getting paid". Marvin shakes his head, "pssssss, man I got a job making good money, tell me where I can buy a car like this." Chucky looks at Marvin, turns up the music, leans back and pulls off fast. Chucky tells Marvin, "It depends on how much money you make." Marvin bragging, "Man I bring home $340 a week."

Chucky starts laughing, "You won't be buying a car like this." Chucky shakes his head and reaches

5

in his pocket and pulls out 3,000 dollars in hundred dollar bills. He puts the money in Marvin's face, "this is money." Marvin eyes opens wide while looking at the money in Chuckey's hand, "hold up man, you got to get me on where you work at." Chucky laughs again, "Cuz I ain't got no job, and I don't need a job. I'm eighteen making five grand a week." "What I need a job for?" Chucky, still smiling at Marvin, "cuz, ima tell you something." "If you want the girls, clothes, a nice ride, you are going to have ta get your hustle on." Marvin, curious, "hustle? Mannnn, you selling drugs now?" Chucky looks at Marvin like he is stupid, "well duhhhh, where else am I going make five grand a week?" "I'm my own boss, and cuz ima tell you the girls be all over me." "Life is good". Marvin looks at Chucky, "you not scared of going to jail?" Chucky shakes his head, "scared? Nah cuz, this is way too easy to get caught. I just pick up, drop off, and then get paid."

During the ride, Marvin is enjoying the attention from everybody staring at them while Chucky continued to talk. They finally arrived at Marvin's job. It's still lunch time and people are outside sitting at the picnic tables eating and socializing. When Chucky pulls up, everyone is staring and talking about his car. Marvin sees a co-worker named Michelle. Marvin has been trying to get

Michelle's attention for months and she never paid him any mind. Marvin points at Michelle while telling Chucky, "that's my future wife right there". Chucky looking up from his cell phone and looks at Michelle, "whoa! She is baddd." Wanting to impress Michelle, Marvin gets out of the car while she was looking. He gives Chucky a pound, "good looking out man, I holla at-cha later." Chucky replies while still looking at Michelle, "no problem cuz, here take my number and give me a call when you're ready to make some real money." Marvin is standing outside the car while adding Chuckey's number to his phone, "nahhhh, that's not for me. That's your thing, I have other plans." Marvin walks up the sidewalk to his job, passes Michelle and hears someone say, "how you doing." Marvin turns around and it was Michelle standing with her arms folded. "Hey Michelle, I'm good. How you doing?" Michelle, chewing gum, "I'm good too, ay who car was that?" Marvin, still trying to impress Michelle, makes up something, "oh that's my cousin's car, and he wants to sell it to me so he brought me to work so I can test it out." Michelle shaking her head up and down and says in a seductive voice, "really? Let me know when you get it, I want a ride." Marvin excited, "you will be the first to know." Then Marvin walked away heading to get his check and sees another co-worker name Renee. Renee and Marvin been friends since elementary school and their families attend the same church. Renee has a crush on Marvin, but Marvin has no idea and treats her like one of his guy friends. Marvin speaks to Renee. "Hey Renee, what's up?" Renee waves her hand with a smirk on her face, "she going to be all over you now." Marvin is confused and looks at Renee, "what you talking about?" "You know, Michelle. Miss High Maintenance. If you get that car she will be all over you." Marvin smiles, "I knowwwwwww!" Renee shakes her head with a smirk on her face in frustration, "I can't believe you guys." Marvin's still confused about Renee's actions, "what's wrong now?" "Y'all don't want someone that likes you for you; y'all rather have a girl that only wants you for what you got". Marvin puts his hands up, "hold that thought Renee, I have to cash my check, talk to you later."

While walking away from Renee, Marvin starts to think about getting a car so he can take out Michelle. He starts to think about what Chucky said about how easy it is to make a lot of money. Without a second thought Marvin grabs his cell phone and calls Chucky. The phone rings and rings with no answer. He hangs up and begins to think that maybe it's good that Chucky didn't answer the phone. Marvin starts to put his phone away and then suddenly it rings. Marvin answers,

"Hello." "Yo, did somebody call Chucky?" Marvin hesitates, "hey Chucky, it's me Marvin, I need to holla at you." Chucky's curious, "aight, what up?" Marvin speaking nervously, "ahhh, I don't want to talk on the phone, but I need to make some money. I mean real money." He's shocked to hear from Marvin so soon, "ohhhh, so you ready to get down huh? I thought it wasn't for you." Chucky's being sarcastic, "I'm only going to do it for a lil while, enough to buy a car. You said it was easy, right?" Chucky takes a deep breath, "I got you cuz, I holla at you tomorrow." Marvin, still not sure, "ok, yeah uhmmm, come by my house tomorrow morning." "Later, cuz."

The next day.

Its 8:15 Saturday morning and Marvin is still in bed sleep. His cell phone rings. Marvin jumps up, reaches over to his nightstand and answers his cell phone. "Hello? Hello?" Marvin's wiping his eyes half asleep. "Yo! Wake up cuz." "Who's this?" "It's me, Chucky wake up! What you wanna do cuz? You still tryna holla at me?" Marvin looks over at the clock. "Yeah, but its 8 o'clock in the morning." "I know what time it is. I got a date later, so holla at me now." Marvin's stretching and yawning, "aight, come on." "Bet, I'll be there in twenty minutes." Marvin hangs up his cell phone and turned back over and closed his eyes. Five minutes went by and Marvin is struggling getting out of bed. He makes his way to the bathroom and washed his face. Marvin then goes back in his bedroom and throws on a pair of sweatpants and a t-shirt and walked up the hallway to the front door. He smells food coming from the kitchen. His mother is cooking breakfast and hears Marvin at the front door. "Marvin, where are you going this early in the morning?" Thinking of something quick to say, "Ahhhhhh, nowhere. I'm looking out for Chucky. He's letting me borrow some play station games." "Well, breakfast is almost ready. So wash your face and hands. Your father wants you to help him today at the church. Marvin disgusted shakes his head, "deggg, what time?" "I don't know. He's over your grandmothers now working on her car. Just make yourself available." "Okayyyyy". Still looking out the front door, Marvin sees an old beat up pickup truck pull up in front of the house and park. He sees Chucky getting out of the passenger side with a back pack hanging on his shoulder. While watching Chucky walking up to the door, Marvin grins and opens the door. Slapping hands and shoulder bumping Marvin looks at the pickup truck, "whats up man?" "Who you riding with?" Yo, you remember my cousin Bobby? Err body calls him BB." "Oh yeahhhhh, I remember BB, what he been up to?" "Same ole same, he drives me around when I'm dirty." Chucky smells the food cooking in the kitchen and rubs his stomach, "cuz what's burning in the kitchen?" "That's moms, you know she be doing her thing." Chucky yells into the kitchen, "Good morning Mrs. Anderson." Marvin's mother heard Chucky, "hi Chucky, how's your mother?" "She's doing ok Mrs. Anderson." "Good, tell her I said hi." "Ok, I will." Chucky looks over at Marvin, "come on, let's get this over with." Marvin started walking down the hall to his bedroom with Chucky behind him. Marvin closed the door and Chucky sat down at the computer desk. Marvin sat on the edge of the bed with his hands in the air, "aight, what's up?" Chucky took the backpack off his shoulder and looks at Marvin, "What you want?" Marvin, looking lost puts his hands up again, "man, I'm trying to make some money, but I don't know what to do." Chucky shakes his head, "cuz calm down, I got you. It's easy, you buy and you sell." Marvin puts his hands on his head, "sell? Sell to who? I don't know nobody that uses this stuff." "Cuz, let me tell you something. You will be surprised whose getting high out here. When they find out that you got it they will come to you. You don't have to worry about finding them." Chucky's feeling hesitant about giving Marvin anything, "I tell you what cuz, start off with

11

something small and see how it works out. If you do good, then go big. But for now give me two-fifty for this." Chucky reaches into his backpack and pulled out several bags of cocaine. Chucky hands Marvin one of those bags. "Ok cuz, try one bag for now and you can double your money, then get back at me." Marvin still confused, "what am I supposed to do with this?" He shakes his head and laughs, "look you're going to double your money. This is how it works... the more you spend the more you make." Chucky sits beside Marvin on the edge of the bed. "I'm going to show you how to get paid." After a half hour of explaining to Marvin on how to double his money, Chucky leaves to get ready for his date.

Marvin is feeling excited while thinking about the money he's going to make. He looks at the bag of cocaine smiling until he realizes he doesn't know anybody that he can sell it too. Now he's worried and wondering if he made the wrong decision. Then he hears his mom calling him, "Marvin!" "Coming". Marvin puts the bag of cocaine under his pillow and ran out his room to see what his mom wants. Marvin walks in the kitchen, "yes ma'am?" Marvin's mother is fixing Marvin a plate of food. "Call over your grandmother's house and see what time your father wants me to bring you by the church." "Yes ma'am." Marvin picks up his cell phone. While making the call, Marvin thinks about his cousin Louis that lives with his grandmother. He might know some people that can buy his cocaine. Louis is a sixteen year old junior at his high school. He has plans to go in the military after he graduates. Louis has a seventeen year old sister named Lisa. They both live with their grandmother. Their father and Marvin's father are brothers. Louis and Lisa parents divorced when they were 2 and 3 years old. Their mother went in the military and remarried, she was never heard from again. Their father became an alcoholic after the divorce, so he left the kids with their grandmother. Meanwhile Marvin thinks Louis can help him get rid of his cocaine because Louis hangs out a lot and knows the streets. Marvin calls Louis. He's listening to the phone ring six times and gets impatient until he hears his grandmother, "hello." "Hey, grandma, this Marvin." "Hi baby, how you doing?" Marvin rushing his grandmother off the phone, "I'm good grandma. I'm looking for dad to find out what time he wants me to meet him at the church." "Your father is still working on my car. I don't think he's going to make it by the church today." Marvin's eyes open wide. Hoping his grandmother is right about not going by the church, "I hope you're right grandma. I have something to do today anyway." "Do whatever you have to do because I have some other things for your father to take care of while I finally got him here." Marvin jumps up, "Yes! Thanks grandma I really need to take care of something. Is Louis up?" "I guess he's up, I hear music coming from his room, hold on I get him." "Thanks grandma, talk to you later". Grandma put the phone down and walked down the hall. She knocked on Louis bedroom door, "Louis, you up? Marvin's on the phone and wants to talk to you." Louis answers while still half way sleep, "ok grandma." Marvin hears Louis stretching and moaning while picking up the phone, "yo, whats up?" "Man you still in the bed?" Marvin asked Louis. "Yeah, me and Troy went out last night. We got in about 4 this morning." "Wake up man, I need you to help me out with something, but can't talk on the phone. I'll be over later and holla at you then." "Aight bet, is everything alright tho?" Yeah, yeah, yeah, I'll holla at you when I get there." Marvin hangs up the phone, and starts getting dressed, and Louis went back to sleep.

Three hours later.

Marvin is in his room playing video games and he looks at his cell phone to see what time it is. Seeing 12:30pm, he turns the game off and went into the living room where his mom is folding clothes. Marvin looks at his mother. "Mom, can you take me to grandma's house?" "I told you I will take you after I finish folding these towels." Another hour went by until they arrived at grandma's house. While pulling up to the house, Marvin sees his father still working on his grandmother's car. He jumps out the car before his mother could turn the car off. Marvin shouts under the car, "Hey dad, what's up?" and kept walking into the house. Marvin's father hears Marvin and shouts back, "hey Marvin, hand me that flashlight on the table. Where's your mother?" "She's coming." "Hey, you're not going by the church this late, are you?" "Nah I don't think so, it's getting late, and your uncle Kevin wants us to come over his house tonight." "Ok good." Before his father could finish talking Marvin took off running into the house to look for Louis. He sees his grandmother getting ready to cook dinner, "hey grandma." "Hi Marvin." Marvin looking around the house, "hey Grandma where's Louis?" "Louis and Troy went to the store for Lisa." "Where's Lisa?" "She and Michael are downstairs watching a movie." "Michael stays here now don't he? He's here more than me."

After talking to his grandmother, Marvin feeling upset, walks out on the porch and calls Louis on the cell phone. Louis answers, "yo, what's up?"

"Man where are you, I'm at grandma's house now." "Man calm down, we almost at the house." "Aight man, hurry up." Ten Minutes later, as Marvin's on the couch watching TV, he hears Louis and Troy coming in the house. Louis walks in the living room, "man what's up, what's so important that you can't talk on the phone? Marvin shakes his head, and puts his figure over his mouth, "Shhhhh, let me talk to you in the bedroom." Marvin looks at Troy, "Troy we'll be back." Marvin got up and followed Louis upstairs to his room. Walking in the bedroom Louis is curious now, "alright what's up?" Marvin not answering closed the door. Louis with a curious look on his face, "man what's up, what's goin on?" Marvin pulls the bag of cocaine out of his pocket and throws it on the bed, "this is what's up." Louis staring at the bag, "What's that?" "Crack cocaine." "I know what it is, but what are you doing with it?" "What you think, we about to get paid." Louis picks up the bag and looks at Marvin, "do you know what ya doing." "Not really, but I just need to find some people that wants to buy it, this is where you come in." Louis getting excited thinking about making money, "man let's do dis." Marvin is happy to hear Louis say that, "cool, then we can be partners, I have a connect that can

16

supply us with whatever we want, he said the more we spend the more we can make." Marvin holding up the bag, "Look let's get rid of this and get more." Louis standing in the middle of the room rubbing his hands together, and shaking his head while listening to Marvin. Louis and Marvin both are excited. All they can think about now is making money. Going back down stairs, they both are excited walking into the living room where Troy is, Louis brags to Troy, "Troy we're about to get paid slim." Troy smiles, "for real, what's up?" Marvin looks at Louis, "what you doing?" Louis throws up his hands, "What? Come on man how are you going to get rid of it if you don't tell no body you got it, plus Troy's cool he's like family and besides he knows where we can get rid of it today." Marvin smiles, "he does, ok let's do it what are we waiting for."

Troy took Marvin and Louis to a neighborhood that was known for selling drugs, within one hour the bag was empty. Excited about making five hundred dollars in one hour, they are looking at each other with disbelief and how easy it was. After selling everything, Marvin noticed that people were still coming to them looking for more. Wanting to make more money they decided to get two bags this time and sell it before it gets late. So Marvin calls Chucky, "Chucky, what's up man I need to holla at you again." "Cuz I told you I was on a date." "Man I'm over here on the avenue and I need that now, people are waiting for it." Chucky laughing, "Oh boy I know that sound, you're hooked, ok I'll meet you in a half hour at the carryout on the ave."

Marvin, Louis, and Troy are at the carry out playing video games waiting for Chucky. Marvin checked the time on his cell phone and thirty minutes went by, and no signs of Chucky. Marvin starts to call Chucky's number again then sees his car coming around the corner. Marvin leaves Louis and Troy in the carryout, and ran outside to the car before Chucky could park. Marvin opens the back passenger door and gets in the back seat, and Chucky pulls off and drives around the block. Marvin smiling and excited, "hey what's up man this is too easy." Marvin looks in the passenger seat to see Chucky's date. It was his co-worker Michelle. Feeling disappointed and betrayed Marvin speaks, "hey Michelle." Michelle waves, but doesn't say nothing, then Chucky ask Marvin, "How much you want?" Marvin counting his money, "I have five hundred." Chucky showing off in front of Michelle throws Marvin four bags by mistake. Marvin thinking that he is supposed to get two bags says nothing. Chucky pulls up in front of the carry out, "aight cuz, I holla at ya later." Marvin, staring at Michelle, "later man." Marvin gets out the car and goes inside the carry-out to get Louis and Troy. Once again they sold everything. This time they made two thousand dollars, now they are really excited. Walking down the street, Louis and Troy are talking about shopping and buying cars, but Marvin is quiet 'cause has other plans.

Its 9:30 at night, Marvin had to go home to get ready for church tomorrow, but before he left, he gave Louis and Troy five hundred dollars apiece and he kept one thousand for himself. Never having that kind of money in his possession before and getting it so easy, and so fast, Marvin is overwhelmed. His mind is racing with all kinds of thoughts and ideas. Marvin gets home and goes straight to his bedroom. He reached in his pocket and pulled out his money. He looks at it again and counts it repeatedly. Then he lies down. Now he is thinking again about how easy and fast it was and that he could make a lot more by selling to dealers, like Chucky. His mind is racing with all kinds of thoughts and plans. He is thinking about going to college and majoring in business, and buying a construction company using the money he makes from selling drugs. Lying in bed counting his money again and again, and with all kinds of thoughts racing through his head, he finally falls asleep.

The next day…

Sunday afternoon, church service had just ended. Pastor Tim reads a message from 1 Peter 5:8. Be alert and of <u>sober</u> mind. Your enemy the devil prowls around like a roaring lion looking for someone to devour. [9] Resist him, standing <u>firm</u> in the faith, because you know that the family of believers throughout the world is undergoing the same kind of sufferings.

Pastor Tim is a forty-five year old single father with a thirteen year old son by his ex-wife Ericka, who left him three years ago because he had a drinking problem. Pastor Tim used to be the lead singer in a R&B music group that played in night clubs all over the city almost every night. He got out of the group and started going to church after being shot at one night by a woman's boyfriend. Now a Pastor, he plans on staying focused and not giving in to temptations. He also has plans on getting his family back. He pastors a small church with eighty members. Every Sunday Pastor Tim gives an awesome message to the congregation. Most of the congregation is up praising and worshipping along with the choir and the lead singer Robin. Robin is a thirty-three year old single lady that has a beautiful voice that she sometimes sings without music, and she also write her own songs. Robin put together a four person gospel band to back her up at the church and other gospel events.

It was the end of service and everybody had left the church. Those that wanted to eat Sunday dinner went over to grandma's house. Sunday's dinner at Grandma's was a tradition. This Sunday it was the family, Pastor Tim, and Lisa had invited Renee over for dinner. Renee caught a ride to grandma's house with Marvin's uncle Kevin and his wife Kim and their kids in their van. Dinner had just ended and everyone is stuffed and sitting around talking. Marvin, Louis, Lisa and Renee, went outside on the porch laughing and joking around, and as usual Louis shows off and pulls out his money and starts counting it. Marvin looks at Louis, "man what are doing?" "Counting my money, what does it look like I'm doing?" Lisa and Renee both put their hands out, "give me some, ooh ooh, give me some money." Marvin can't believe Louis, "man put that away." Louis puts his money back in his pocket, but Lisa and Renee start wondering. "Louis, where you get that money from?" Before Louis says something stupid, Marvin changes the subject, "who feels like walking to the store?" Marvin standing up and waving his hand to Renee, "come on, walk with me to the store." Renee gets up laughing, and Marvin is looking at Louis shaking his head. Marvin and Renee left walking to the store. Conversing about school and work, Renee tells Marvin how she plans on going in the Navy when she graduates, and then they started laughing and joking. Renee having fun walking with Marvin wants to tell him she likes him but don't know how. Then there is a minute of silence. "You know Marvin, I think that you are a nice person and you deserve better than someone like Michelle." Marvin thinks about Michelle and Chucky, "Yeahhhhh, you're right, she's not for me." Renee starting to open up, then her cell phone rings. Looking at her caller ID, "it's Lisa, hello." "Hey girl where yall at, Uncle Kevin is ready to go home." "Ok, I'm on my way. I'll be there in a minute." Minutes later, they got back to the house, and everybody was outside talking and laughing. Kevin and Kim saw Renee, so they started walking to their van. Renee hurries and joins them and gets in the van. Waving bye and thanking grandma for dinner, Renee gets a text message. It's from Marvin (would you like to go to the movies with me). Renee smiling texting back (yes).

Later that night, Marvin is at home on the computer surfing the net, and thinking about turning that thousand dollars into two-thousand dollars. Getting up from his computer to get his cell phone he calls Chucky, but there was no answer. After an hour and several attempts of trying to call Chucky, Marvin stopped trying to call him. Hoping that Bobby might know where Chucky is, Marvin called Bobby. "Yo BB, what's up man?" "Nuttin, just chilling." "Hey man, I been trying to get in touch with your lil cuz Chucky, you heard from him?" "Whatttttt, you didn't hear about what happened, Chucky got shot last night." Marvin shocked, "do what, what happened, is he ok?" "Naaaa he didn't make it, I don't know what happened, I heard he got robbed, man you know Chucky, and he would let everybody know his business." "I tell you what, never let nobody know your business, I mean nobody not even yo momma." Marvin is pacing the floor and puts his hand on his forehead, "nah man, I can't believe this." "Let me tell you something, that's part of the game, it comes with the territory, you live fast, you die young, but anyway if you're looking for anything I got it." "Marvin is confused and can't stop thinking about Chucky, "ok uhmmm, yeah, yeah lets hook up tomorrow."

Five years later...

Marvin is now twenty-three and Louis is twenty-two. They are partners in a drug business that averages thirty to forty thousand dollars a week by selling to street dealers. They can make more money but Marvin only deals with a few people. Louis wants to make more money and is willing to sell to anybody that has a dollar. They share a house in the suburbs part of Maryland in a new small community with only twenty-five new homes. The rental is a 4500 square foot, three level house with four bedrooms, four bathrooms and a three car garage. Behind the house on a half-acre of land surrounded by trees, are a few more houses that are under construction. The neighbors don't suspect anything because Marvin keeps their business away from the house. He arranges to meet his buyers at different meeting locations, except for one buyer name Travis. He trusts Travis because he's low key, and owns a three man crew home improvement company and drives the company truck dressed in work clothes all the time. Travis brings Marvin six thousand dollars a week.

Marvin is the brain behind their drug business. He makes most of the decisions and has plans to start a construction company and get out the drug business, but there are times that he likes the easy money and forgets all about his plans. He has two hundred and twenty thousand dollars in a safe that he keeps in a wall in the basement. His goal is to save up three hundred thousand to help start his construction company. He drives his all white new Mercedes or his new gold and black Range Rover. Marvin is enjoying life because everything is going as planned for him with his third year in college. Taking business courses three day a week and learning the construction field in his spare time, he feels good about the way everything is going. When he's not in school, he is at the gym working out and boxing or he is with his one year old son lil Marvin, by his girlfriend of five years, Renee. Renee doesn't approve of Marvin dealing drugs, so her and lil Marvin lives with her parents. Renee is a fifth grade school teacher, and there isn't a day that goes by that she doesn't ask Marvin to stop selling drugs so that they can get married and be a family.

Louis is the opposite of Marvin; he has no plans of ever stopping. He loves everything about this lifestyle and wants it to last forever. Everywhere he goes he is wide open, and can't nobody tell him nothing. Excited by the money, cars, girls, and street fame he's having a ball. He's always bragging to people about what he got, and what he's going to get. It's because of Marvin that people even respects Louis. Almost every night Louis and his best friend Troy are out partying, gambling or riding around. Louis drives a luxury car, SUV, sports car, or his motorcycle. Marvin and Louis both still stop by their grandparents' house everyday to visit or eat dinner. Grandma still loves to cook. Louis' sister Lisa lives with their grandparents. She has two boys by her ex-boyfriend Michael. Lisa is raising her kids by herself and Michael doesn't help or come to visit the kids. Lisa supports herself and her kids by working as an administrative assistant for a law firm.

Grandma is sixty-nine years old with a loving spirit. It's because of her love for God that she is a giving and kind person. She raised her kids and grandkids all in church. Every night before she goes to sleep she prays for everybody, especially Marvin and Louis. She knows what they are doing. Grandpop is seventy-one years old. He sits back and watches everything but doesn't say much. He likes to mind his business unless someone asks him a question.

Marvin's uncle Kevin is forty-two and his wife Kim is forty. They have two boys, eleven and nine, and a daughter seven years old. It's because of grandma raising her kids in church that Kevin brings his family to church. They never miss a church service or event. Kevin spends a lot of time with his oldest son Jr. and he figures at eleven years old, it's time to put him in activities and raise him to be a responsible man. Wanting to be successful at work, Kevin works hard and plans on becoming a supervisor at a major manufacture company that distributes to retailers. His goal is to one day be the superintendent for the company. Kim is a beautician and she set up a shop in the basement at their house so she could be home with the kids.

Marvin's parents retired in South Carolina and they spend their time traveling. Everyone attends the same church, over the past five years the congregation grew up to one hundred and five people now. Every Sunday the church is packed to hear God's word from Pastor Tim Adams, and afterwards family and friends head over to grandma's house for Sundays dinner.

Meanwhile it's Saturday afternoon, and Travis and his work crew have just pulled up in the driveway at Marvin's house. Travis looks at the guy sitting in the passenger seat, "hey Brian, look in the glove box and hand me that envelope." Brian opens the glove box and saw an open envelope with a stack of money in it, and picks it up and gives it to Travis. Travis is surprised to see the envelope open, "hey you didn't see that alright." Brian just shakes his head yes. Travis stuffed the envelope in his pocket, "it's hot out here guys so give me a second." Travis gets out of the truck and walks up the sidewalk to the door. Louis comes out of the house at the same time dressed in an all-white tee shirt, tan khaki shorts, white flip flops and a white baseball cap turn backwards and wearing a silver chain hanging down to his stomach. Louis meets Travis and they shakes hands and bump shoulders, "What up Louis, where you off too?" "I have to pick up Troy to look at some bikes." "That's what's up, where cuz at?" "Yeah he in there eating that healthy stuff watching the sports channel." Travis' laughing, "yeahhhhh that's Marvin." Travis walks in the house, and Louis walks over to his truck. Travis' work crew was looking at Louis' truck while talking to each other, "hey, how that young boy get a truck like that and live in this house?" Brian turns around and looks in the back seat, "What you think?" I tell you what, man… I'm tired of busting my butt working everyday in this heat and these young boys don't have to work, but have everything." The two guys in the back seat was curious, "hey Brian what was in that envelope that you gave Travis?" "Cuz, a stack of hundred dollar bills." "What! I wish I knew that was in there." Watching Louis as he pulls off, Louis looks back at them and taps his horn while putting on his shades. Brian is curious now. He looked at the guys, "what would you have done if you knew that money was in there?" The two guys in the back seat laughing, "It would have mysteriously come up missing." With a serious look on his face Brian turns around again, "hey it still can mysteriously come up missing, and much more." "I have a plan, what yall tryna do?" Now Travis's crew is sitting in the truck making plans to rob Marvin and Louis. Minutes later Travis walks out the house and gets in the truck and leaves.

The next day…

Its six o'clock Sunday morning. Renee and Lil Marvin fell asleep last night in Marvin's bed after watching movies all night. Renee wakes up with Lil Marvin sleep beside her and looks at the clock. She looks around for Marvin and doesn't see him, so she gets up and walks out the room. She hears the television on in Louis room and walks down stairs. Still no signs of Marvin, then she hears the front open. Marvin walks in breathing heavy, "hey good morning, what you doing up so early?" "I have to go home and get ready for church." "Where you been?" "I went running before it gets hot." "Well I wish you had told somebody, I wake up and you're gone, I didn't know what to think." Marvin walks past Renee and goes into the kitchen to get a bottle of water, "stop worrying all the time." "I'm always worrying as long as you keep selling that junk." "Worried about what?" "You going to jail or get killed or something!" "Oh boy, not now Renee. I'm going up stairs to take a shower. I'll see yall at church."

Hours later…

Everybody is at church and Pastor Tim is giving a message on repentance from Luke 13:2, [2] Jesus answered, "Do you think that these Galileans were worse sinners than all the other Galileans because they suffered this way? [3] I tell you, no! But unless you repent, you too will all perish. Pastor Tim was reading and preaching, "Sin is sin, there is no level for sin, and we must repent from all sin." Once again some people were uplifted, and some heard and forgot what they heard minutes later, and some were talking about whatever to each other.

After service, everyone went their separate ways and after socializing, friends and family went to grandma's house for dinner. Grandma had cooked roast beef, mashed potatoes, cabbage, corn-on-the-cob, and cornbread and she made her famous iced tea that everyone loves. Everybody is standing around the table and Pastor Tim is getting ready to bless the food. While Pastor Tim was praying, Grandma noticed that Marvin wasn't there. After blessing the food Grandma asked, "Has anybody seen Marvin?" She knew he wouldn't miss Sunday's dinner for nothing. Renee and little Marvin was there waiting for him also. Renee walks over to Louis, "hey, where's your big head cousin?" Louis shrugging his shoulders, "I haven't seen Marvin since we left church. He said he needed to run by the house for something and that he'll meet me at Grandma's house."

Louis and Renee both started calling Marvin's cell phone and neither one had got an answer. Curious about Marvin's whereabouts, everybody started eating. They knew he would be there soon. Marvin had gone to meet Bobby to give him a package. Not knowing that Bobby had gotten in trouble Thursday night for selling to an undercover police officer, and to get out of trouble the police told Bobby that he had to set up his supplier. Bobby agreed to work with the detectives to get out of trouble by setting up Marvin.

Yesterday Bobby was up all day and night trying to convince himself to call Marvin. Then he finally gets up the nerve to make the call. It was

Sunday morning, after Marvin got out of the shower, his phone rings, thinking that it was Renee calling to apologize because she had just left the house upset, Marvin answers the phone, "Yes Renee." "Na man, this Bobby." Marvin is surprised, "Bobby, what up?" Bobby, talking nervous, "Nothing much man, what's up with you?" "Same oh same oh, getting ready to go to church," Marvin is puzzled about the phone call so early on Sunday morning. "Ok good, good, I called because I'm going to need that thing from you today". Marvin laughs, "Man its early Sunday morning, you couldn't wait until later to call me? You know I don't do business on Sundays." Bobby trying to think of something fast, "my fault, man I been up all night, so I thought I catch you before you went to church." Marvin looks at his watch and sees that it's getting late for church and start to rush Bobby off the phone, but he's not thinking and tells Bobby, "Ok, ok I'll be by around three or four, after service." "Alright man thanks, I holla at you." Feeling relieved, Bobby hangs up the phone and goes through his wallet looking for the detective's number, so he could let him know what time Marvin is coming over his apartment. Feeling guilty about setting up Marvin, Bobby found the card. Staring at the card, Bobby starts to think about Marvin again, and how close they been for years, then he thinks about going to jail, so he makes the call. "Hello, I need to speak to Detective Morris." "Yes sir speaking, how can I help you?" "Hey man this is Bobby." "I know who this is, I thought I was going to have to come and pick you up, what took you so long?" Then silence. Bobby puts his head down. "Hey Bobby, you there?" Bobby taking a deep breath and blows it out, "yeah yeah, umm I made the call and Marvin will be here at my apartment around three." Before Detective Morris could answer, Bobby hangs up the phone and goes in the bathroom and splash cold water on his face, then looks at himself in the mirror.

It was the end of church service, and Marvin went back to his house to pick up the package that Bobby asked for. Feeling hungry, he calls Bobby before he leaves, and gets no answer, so he leaves a message. "Hey Bobby, I'm on my way, and I'm in a hurry man you know Grandma is cooking Sunday dinner, and I'm starving so call me back." It's almost three o'clock and Marvin pulled up in front of Bobby's apartment, he parked his car. Looking around to see how things look, Marvin gets out his car and goes into the back seat and grabbed his back pack. Putting the back pack on one shoulder, he closes the door and hits the car door lock button on his key chain, and starts to walk towards the apartment building. Marvin sees a small car come in the parking lot, a plain car with a couple of guys laughing and joking. The car stopped to let Marvin cross the road to enter the building. The two men in the car are undercover police officers. Marvin walked across the road waving thanks to the men. Not thinking anything is wrong, he keeps going and in front of him, coming out of the apartment building were three men laughing and talking, so Marvin kept walking. Marvin started up the steps and once he had gotten within arm's reach of the detectives they tackled him, and the other two detectives in the car jumped out with their guns drawn and screaming "lay on the ground! Don't move". One of the undercover officers went straight to the back pack, opened it and found the drugs, it was five ounces of cocaine, "we gotcha now buddy." Marvin's on the ground shaking his head, while repeatedly screaming Bobbie's name, "BOBBY, BOBBY, what's up man?" "I can't believe you did this to me, we supposed to be like family man." Bobby is sitting in the back seat of the car watching and listening to

Marvin screaming his name. The detectives snatched Marvin up off the ground by the handcuffs. One detective took the back pack with the drugs and another detective took Marvin by the arm and put him in the back seat of a separate car. The one detective got in the driver's seat and looked at Marvin in the rear mirror, "Ok you know how this works, you work for us now or go to jail." Marvin shaking his head, "man I know nothing, so take me to jail".

Travis' work crew is going through with their plan to rob Marvin. Brian made a copy of Travis' truck keys while he and two co-workers had stolen Travis' work truck and drove it to Marvin's house. They parked in the driveway waiting for Marvin to come home. They are hoping that Marvin will think that Travis is in the truck with them and he will come over to the truck. They have guns and rope and they have no plans for Marvin to be alive when they finish.

Meanwhile at grandma's house, dinner was over two hours ago and everyone went home. The family was still wondering what happened to Marvin. He never misses Sunday's dinner. Scared now that something might be wrong, Louis walked outside to make some phone calls and hears the news about what happened, to Marvin. Hanging up the phone, he grabs his head. Louis' mind is racing and he starts feeling scared and lost, he hesitates to tell the family about what he heard, but knows he has to. Walking back in the house, Louis takes a deep breath and blows, "look yall, Marvin got locked up." Everyone is shocked and upset and asking questions, "what, what happened?" Louis is nervous and scared, wondering if the police are looking for him, but he tries not to show that he is scared by joking around. Renee broke down crying and grabbed Lil Marvin and left.

Later that night the phone rings and Lisa runs to pick it up, "hello." A machine asks Lisa if she will accept a collect phone call from the county jail, if so push one. Lisa accepts the call, "hey Marvin, how are you? And you know I can't be accepting phone calls from jail on grandma's phone." Marvin talking fast, "I know, I won't be long, I'm sure everyone heard by now what happened." Lisa smacking her lips, "yeah I can't believe Bobby, are you ok?" Angry, Marvin answers, "I'm good, I know a couple of people in here, but how is Renee and what did grandma say?" "Renee is really upset, she is taking it hard, and grandma was jumping on Louis, telling him he is going to jail next, if he doesn't get his self together. "Where is Louis?" "He went over Troy's. He scared to go home." "Tell him he can go home, it happened at Bobby's apartment, not the house." "Ok I'll tell him tomorrow, let him be scared for a while." A line of people is waiting to use the phone behind Marvin. "Tell everybody I'm ok and I'll talk to them later, tell Louis I need to talk to him about getting a lawyer and bond money. I have to go; other people need to use the phone. Hey tell Renee I love her and its going to be ok, got to go, bye". Marvin hangs up the phone and goes to his room, feeling bad about Renee taking it hard he lays down.

Three months later, Marvin is still in jail. He was denied bond because he won't work with the detectives to set up his supplier. Today is his court date, and Grandma, Renee and Pastor Tim came to court to support him. Because he was caught with the drugs on him, Marvin's lawyer suggested that he plead guilty to possession with the intent to distribute. With the plea bargain and turning over his car, truck and any possessions that are in his name, the Judge gave Marvin 10 years and suspends 5. He has to do 5 years before he comes home. Renee gets upset again and starts crying while yelling, "Marvin why, why? I told you, I told you, and what about little Marvin, what are we going to do?" Marvin hangs his head down, and is scared thinking about Renee and Marvin Jr. The Judge looks at Renee and allows Marvin to go talk to her before going to prison. Marvin hugs Renee, "It's going to be okay. Five years will go by in no time, come on Renee I need you to be strong now. I promise you when I come home this life is over for me." Renee can't stop crying, "Okay." Then Grandma, Renee, Pastor Tim, and Marvin held hands and said a prayer for Marvin that he will use this time wisely and build a relationship with God. They started hugging and saying their goodbyes. Pastor Tim and Grandma left the court building, Renee stayed with Marvin until he had to go back to jail.

On the way to take Grandma home, Pastor Tim tells Grandma, "I need to go by the church. I forgot something." They pulled up in front of the church and Pastor Tim ran in and out. When he got back in the car, he made a phone call to Robin, the leader of the choir. There's no answer so he left a message. "Hello Robin, this is Pastor Tim. I have your check with me; call me when you get this message." Grandma heard Pastor Tim say Robins name, "let me tell you that girl can sing! She had people crying Sunday, she has really been gifted". Pastor Tim, agreeing with Grandma, "Yes God has blessed her with a great voice". Finally getting to Grandma's house, they saw Kevin and Jr. on the porch with Grandpop. Grandma got out the car and started up the steps to the porch. Concerned about Marvin, Kevin asked Grandma "how did Marvin make out?" Grandma comes walking up the steps, "he has to do five years." "And what are you doing home? Didn't you have to work today?" "No I took off; I had to take Jr. to the doctor today." Grandma's worried about Jr., "oh is my baby ok?" "Yes maam, he's fine, he's playing sports now so he had to get a physical." Still worried about Marvin being in jail, Grandma started thinking about Louis, "Y'all seen Louis?" "I thought he would have come to court to see Marvin." Kevin is surprised Louis didn't go to court. "No, we haven't heard from him, I thought he was with you." Now that Marvin is in jail, Louis doesn't come around the family much. He doesn't have time.

After Louis heard that the police wasn't looking for him, he moved on and started doing business on his own with the money that Marvin had saved up. He has three guys hanging with him that he calls his crew, Troy is his main man. You see one, you see the other; and the other two guys, Scoota and Fat Frank, are neighborhood friends. Doing things without Marvin, Louis is living fast. He is making more money than before because he sells to anybody and everybody that has a dollar. Louis now averages fifty thousand a week by himself. Louis didn't make it to Marvin's court appearance because he and Troy went to Atlantic City for the weekend and didn't get home until that morning. Louis and Troy spends a lot of time and money shopping, gambling, partying, attending sports events and taking trips. Louis even bought an RV for when him and his crew travels together.

One month later.

Marvin was taken to a prison where he will spend the next four and a half years. He's in his room putting up pictures of Renee and Lil Marvin on the wall beside his pillow, and organizing his clothes while trying to make these four years comfortable. Walking out of his room Marvin looks around, to the left a television is hanging on the wall with a group of chairs in front of it. He looks to his right and sees two pool tables and a bunch of tables, and the guard booth is straight ahead. He walks outside to see what's out there. When he gets outside he sees two more buildings, one says cafeteria and the other says gym. Walking over to the gym to see what's in there and ready to work out, he figures working out will keep his mind occupied and stay in shape at the same time. When he gets inside the gym he sees a couple of people, but most of the inmates are outside in the yard. He picks up a basketball and starts to shoot hoops for a while, and then someone calls him. "Hey, hey buddy you got a minute?" Marvin points at himself, "you talking to me?" "Yeah, I need a spot." "You got a minute?" Marvin throws the ball at the basket, "yeah yeah yeah, I got you." Marvin runs over to the weights and stands behind the bench and helps this guy lift his last rep. The guys sits up on the bench, "ahh, thanks man that's it for me, I'm finished." "No problem." "Hey I never saw you before you new around here?" "Yeahhhhh, I just got here." Sitting on the bench with his hand out, "Ok well welcome to the pen, young man I'm Leon." Marvin shaking his head with a smirk on his face and being sarcastic, "Yeahhhhh thanks." "I tell you what young blood, keep your nose clean around here and you be ok. Don't get caught up in the dumb stuff and watch your crowd." "Thanks for the info, good looking out."

Leon is a fifty years old Jamaican man and has two years left to serve of his ten year sentence. He is a major drug dealer from New York that a lot of people fear because of his reputation on getting people killed that crossed him. Leon and his family made millions selling drugs and they own a couple of car dealerships. Leon looks at Marvin while he's taking off his gloves, "are you here at this time every day?" "I can be, I ain't got nowhere to go for the next couple of years." Marvin's laughing. Walking out the gym Leon looks back, "alright man, we'll get it in tomorrow."

Three weeks later.

After breakfast, Marvin is jogging around the yard and listening to music on his headphones, he looks through the fence at the trees that surround the prison, and he starts to think about home, Lil Marvin and Renee. Then he stops running, and it hits him, he's locked up and his family is out there without him and he should be with them and not locked up. Thinking about Renee and little Marvin, he stopped running and went back into the building. Still thinking about Renee, he wants to talk to her but both phones were tied up, so he goes to his room to get ready to take a shower and change his clothes.

Later that day Marvin went over to Leon's room, this is Marvin first time going to someone else's room. When Marvin got to Leon's room, he knocked on the door and yells, "Yo Leon." Leon walks out his room, "hey young man, come on in, I'm just watching TV." Marvin walks inside of Leon's room and sees a twenty eight inch color TV with a DVD and CD player, then he looks at the pictures of Leon and his family, cars and girl's and stacks of letters in a box in the corner, after looking at Leon pictures Marvin knew right away that Leon was making money. Marvin is curious, "Man what type of work you do?" "Why you ask?" "Lookin at these pictures, it looks like you was getting paid." "I own a couple of car lots. I'm a business man Marvin." "Oh aight, it must be nice." "It is, plus a lil extra on the side." Marvin knows what extra means. He looks at a picture with Leon and a lady both wearing fur coats and

Leon has on a gold chain with diamonds in it. "Man, can I make a lil extra on the side?" "Of course, there's lots of money out there for everybody." "You know anything about the game Marvin?" "Yeah, that's why I'm here, a so-called friend set me up." Leon starts to laugh, "A friend? Yo that's no friend Marvin. First rule in this game is you don't have no friends, and don't trust anyone, not even family." "Where are you from?" "Maryland." "Oh yeahhhhh, I can make you a rich man." Marvin and Leon sat down, while Leon was asking Marvin a lot of questions about Maryland and how was his drug business. They talked for hours, and now they're making plans to hook up when they get out of prison. Realizing the time Marvin jumped up, "man it's getting late I'm going to go get ready for chow." As Marvin started walking out of the room, Leon puts his arm up and stopped him, "oh yeah my friend, we never had this conversation ok." Marvin, looking at Leon and sees a very serious face, "and never cross me." Marvin sees the seriousness on Leon's face, "Naaaa, you don't have to worry about me, I'm about making money."

Its dinner time and Marvin is headed for the cafeteria. Walking into the crowded cafeteria, Marvin looks around for Leon, but doesn't see him, so he gets in line. Standing in line holding his tray, Marvin grabs a fork and a spoon then feels a tap on his shoulder. It was an older man named James Trolley standing in line behind him. James' nick name at the prison is Rev. Rev is forty-seven years old and serving a life sentence at the prison. They call him Rev because he likes to have church in his room and talks to people about the word of God all the time. Some of the guys at the prison think Rev is crazy because he praises God out loud at times in his room by himself. Rev has church in his room twice a week with other inmates, normally 7 to 9 people attends, but all is invited. Standing in the food line behind Marvin Rev taps Marvin on the shoulder. Marvin turns around with an angry look, and Rev puts his hands up out and smiles, "hello young man, how are you today?" Marvin looks at Rev, "you talking to me?" Rev humbles himself, "yes sir, I notice that you're new around here and I just like to introduce myself, my name is James but everyone calls me Rev." Marvin gets defensive. "Yeah, no disrespect Rev, but I'm not trying to meet nobody, the less people I know, the better off I am." Rev sees that

Marvin is getting defensive and steps back smiling, "I understand, I don't mean you no harm young man I just wanted to introduce myself." "Well you did that now you can leave me alone." Rev puts his hands up again and smiles, "Ok I understand, but I have some information that can help your stay here a peaceful one if you want it." Acting sarcastic Marvin jumps on Rev, "information, information about what?" "Man you don't know me, why you want to give me helpful information, look man I don't want nothing from you so stop talking to me." Marvin mocking Rev, "I got information, if you got information why don't you use it and get out of here." Rev, still not giving up, "I do have some useful information, instructions on life, but it's your choice if you want it or not." Laughing Marvin turns around with his back to Rev "did you say instructions on life, yeah I hear ya old man." Marvin shaken his head thinking Rev is crazy, "look here pops I had enough, now I told you to leave me alone." Marvin turns around and continues to walk in line. Marvin gets his food and walks away from Rev and finds a seat at a crowded table, and Rev gets out of line and leaves the cafeteria hoping that he left Marvin with something to think about.

Only eating half of his food, Marvin gets up and empties his tray into the trash can and heads back to his room to read his mail. He opens a letter from Renee. Smiling while looking at pictures of little Marvin and reading his letter, his eyes starts to get watery. Marvin gets a letter everyday from Renee, letting him know how everyone is doing, but hasn't heard from Louis. Louis and his crew are busy hanging out every night. Later that night, notices the phone is free decides to call Grandma's house. Lisa answers the phone and talks to Marvin about Louis and his crew, "Marvin, Louis is wide open. He wears diamond earrings, a long white gold chain down to his stomach, and has a matching watch and ring." "That stuff is worth at least fifteen to twenty thousand dollars." "Woe, he is really showing off, tell him he better be careful out there." "OK Marvin it's getting late and I have to put the kids to bed. Oh yeah, I saw Travis and he said that Brian and his other employees had planned on robbing you the day you got locked up, and they had guns and rope." "What?"

Before he could say something, Marvin hears loud voices and shouting coming from Rev's room. Rev's room is about a hundred feet away from the phone. After talking to Lisa, Marvin sat down at a table in the middle of the dorm, and joined in a card game. Twenty minutes later he watched a group of guys come out of Rev's room looking happy, rejoicing, laughing, and in a good mood. Watching these guys rejoicing coming out of Rev's room made him curious about what's going on in there, and wondering why are they so happy being in prison. The other inmates already knows what is going on, they're used to it. Curious, he gets up and walks past Rev's room. While passing by his room Marvin tries to peep inside to see what was so exiting, but he doesn't stop he keeps on walking. He didn't see anything that would make these guys act like they did, so he turns back around and tries to look again and still doesn't see nothing exciting, but this time when he walks by Rev comes to the door way and calls him, "Young man, can I help you?" "You know it's not polite to peep in other people rooms around here." Marvin still curious tells Rev. "Yeah, my fault, but I was wondering was everything ok over here." "I saw some guys come out here laughing, all happy and stuff, it looks like a party going on over here Rev." Rev, acting like Marvin doesn't know what he is missing, "there is a party going on son, we're rejoicing about getting this knowledge that I was telling you about earlier, so life can't keep us locked up no matter where we are or what the circumstances are, we will rejoice at all times." Rev's jumping up and down shouting, "you see me in prison, but I'm free Marvin, I'm free." "What you talking about Rev?" Rev feels like the door had just been opened to talk to Marvin about God, "I'm free because of Jesus, He died for me and you." "The enemy doesn't want you to know that, he wants us to walk around mad, down, and depressed so he can control your life." "Young man, get control of your life, get out of prison!" Rev said pointing at Marvin's head. Marvin wants to ask how; instead he asked Rev, "I do have control of my life." "Son, right now you don't have control of your life, something else is controlling you, and you don't know it, it could be people, jobs, money, or even yourself. That's why you are in prison mentally and physically." "God did not create you to be in prison physically or mentally, because you can be home and still be in prison in your mind." Rev's pointing at Marvin's head again. "You need to change the way you think and be transformed by renewing your mind. Read and follow the instruction, rules, and the order on how to live so you could have life, and not life having you." Rev pulls out his Bible and shows it to Marvin. "Here it is, all you need to know on how to live. Follow these instructions, rules, and the order it's supposed to be in and you too can be free." Marvin gets a smirk on his face, "oh you been talking about the bible, man I was raised in church, I go to church every Sunday." "I know the Bible." Marvin started saying scriptures to Rev. Rev, surprised, tells Marvin, "let me show you something." Rev started turning the pages in his Bible, "read this 2 Timothy 3:15." [15] You have been taught the Holy Scriptures from childhood, and they have given you the wisdom to receive the salvation that comes by trusting in Christ Jesus. [16] All Scripture is inspired by God and is useful to teach us what is true and to make us realize what is wrong in our lives. It corrects us when we are wrong and teaches us to do what is right. [17] God uses it to prepare and equip his people to do every good work. Rev looks at Marvin, "This is you!" Rev tells Marvin with a serious face and strong voice "Son, its people like you that make me angry, you know Gods word, but you still choose to live your way. It's like driving a car against traffic down the street and you read the one-way sign, but you choose to drive in the wrong direction anyway because you want to. Now you know you're driving against traffic so it's only a matter of time before you crash. But you are the driver and God gave you the power to turn that car around and go the right way so you won't crash. So you have a choice to make, either keep going against traffic and crash or make a u-turn; that means repent. The choice is yours son. I tell you what, meet me back here tomorrow at 5:30. You have a choice to make and God is going to use me to help you." Rev hands Marvin a Bible, "take this, this is yours. Before you go to sleep tonight read Proverbs 3:5-6, believe it, and meditate on it." Marvin shakes Revs hand, and thanked him for that message. There's an hour left before bed time so Marvin goes over to watch TV. While watching TV, Marvin starts to think about what Rev told him. He starts to think about that car as his life going the wrong direction heading for a crash, and he read the one-way sign.

The next day at 5:25, Marvin walks over to Rev's room with his Bible in his hand. Marvin sees a neighborhood friend named Paul running down the steps calling his name. "Marvin, Marvin." Almost at Rev's room Marvin hears Paul and turns around. Paul tries to catch his breath. "Marvin, glad to see you man. These jokers trying to jump me over a $200 bet. Man you gotta help me out." Trying not to get mixed up in it, Marvin shakes his head.

"Man what you doing making bets in this place? Just pay up and get it over with." Paul is scared. "That's the problem, I can't pay up. I lost all my money gambling. Man you got my back right, we from around the way. Boy I'm glad to see you, come on walk with me to my room." Marvin looks at the clock and its 5:30, his mind is racing. He thinks about Rev and he's thinking that if he lets Paul get jumped, he's wrong for that because they are from the same neighborhood, and what the guys around the way are going to think. At this time Rev walks out his room and sees Marvin talking to his Paul. Rev sees that something is wrong and calls Marvin. "Marvin, Marvin what you going to do? Are you going to help me with this situation or what?" Marvin, not wanting to go with Paul, is happy to see Rev and plays along with him. "Yeah Rev, ahhh I be there in a minute." Marvin explains to Paul, "Man, I told Rev I would help him out at 5:30. Look, just tell them you will pay them and I'll give you the money." Paul is wondering what Marvin is doing, because he would normally be ready to fight. "What, man these guys gonna get me. We from around the way, what's up?" Marvin throws his hands up, "I told you I'll give you the money." "Man forget Rev, we supposed to have each

53

other's back." Now he wants to get away from Paul. "I tell you what, tell them to come see me and I will pay your bet off but that's it! Stop making bets that you can't pay, and don't be dragging me in your mess man." Paul shaking Marvin's hand, "cool, good looking out, I'll pay you back soon as I get some money." Marvin knows he won't see that $200 again, but it's worth getting Paul away from him.

Marvin walks over to Rev's room. He thinks Rev is upset with him. "Sorry about that Rev, that's one of the guys from around my way." Rev smiling, "What you sorry about, you did nothing wrong. Besides I knew this was going to happen." Marvin looks at Rev, "You did, how?" "Because, the devil doesn't want you to get this word, so he will put obstacles in the way to stop you. He used your friend this time, and there will be a next time, and a next. It could be anything or person. You just have to make the right decision when you are faced with these obstacles. The closer you get to God, the harder the devil is going to work, so let's get started." Marvin is looking around. "Hey where is everybody?" "It's just you and me; I asked the other guys if they would meet somewhere else." Marvin asks Rev, "Why, what's up?" Rev explains. "I prayed and God wants us to have a one-on-one, because you have a little over three years before you go home and you need to be transformed by renewing your mind before you hit the streets. It is in the streets that you are faced with temptations. You will have to think different, see things different, you will be a new creature in Christ. God is using me to help you renew your mind, changing the way you think is the beginning, everything you do begin in the mind." Marvin is curious. "Hold up Rev, how you know I have a little over three years to go home, I never told nobody." Rev closes his Bible and starts telling Marvin about his job around the jail. Well, I work in the data info room and I put new comer's data in the computer, and short timers like yourself I believe God wants to use me to help you become a new creature in the name of Jesus before you go back in the streets, by sharing his word and instructions with you. A lot of guys get locked up and find God, but when they get out they get away from Gods plan and come right back in here, we are going to keep you out of here." Rev with a serious look on his face, "Let me tell you something, you getting locked up, and sitting here with me learning Gods plan for you, is no mistake. If you had stayed in the streets you could be dead by now." When Rev said that Marvin started to think about the day he got locked up and Brian was waiting to rob him. "Woe, you're right Rev. some dudes were going to kill me the day I got locked up."

"Ok let get started, tell me little about yourself. Are you married with kids?" Putting up his left hand, showing no rings, "Na I'm not married, I mean not yet I have a girlfriend that I plan to marry one day and we have a son." "Well you have to make a change for yourself and your son. And who knows, you might get married one day and raise your family, but you need help from God. You can't do it without him." Opening his Bible, Rev asks Marvin some questions to see where he is, "do believe in God and that Jesus died for you and your sins?" "Yeah, but sometimes no, I mean I don't know." Holding up his hands, "Sometimes I believe, sometimes I don't." "Why you feel sometimes you don't believe? What makes you feel like that?" Marvin throws his hands up again, "look around, all that's going on. How come God lets these things happen? I mean all you see is wrong."

Rev says a prayer before they start reading. "It's time you learn about faith so you can believe what you read, and know that this is a word from God. Now all of the answers to your questions will come from God not me, so let's open the Bible." Rev gives Marvin an ink pen and paper. "You said all you see is the wrong that's around you. Let's go to 2 Corinthians 4:4, it says." The god of this age has blinded the minds of unbelievers, so that they cannot see the light of the gospel that displays the glory of Christ, who is the image of God. "The devil blinds you by showing you nothing but the wrong that's around you so that you can't see the goodness of God. But the devil is the master of lying and deceiving, so take off the blind fold and get the truth. Read your Bible. Start looking at the blessing that's around you. There are so many blessings that we look at as problems and don't realize that it's a blessing because we are not getting the truth. If you see with your eyes, you are easy to be fooled." Rev gives Marvin examples of the world lies and what the truth says. Then he tells Marvin, "Now go to Hebrews 11:1." Faith is the substance of things hoped for, the evidence of things not seen. "See you have to believe and know what you believe is real, it's all about having faith."

Rev starts giving Marvin examples of faith and how it is used in everyday life. "You must put action along with your faith, read James 2:26 it says." [26]For as the body without the spirit is dead, so faith without works is dead also. "So you have to put in work with your faith." Marvin enjoyed learning how to relate the Bible to his life. He never looked at the Bible like that. Although he went to church every Sunday and heard the word of God, he was never taught how to read the Bible to live. Rev tells Marvin, "read and pray that God gives you the understanding on what you are reading, tonight read Hebrews 11:6. It says, "And without faith it is impossible to please God, because anyone who comes to him must believe that he exists and that he rewards those who earnestly seek him. "BELIEVING is the key."

Five weeks later.

Rev and Marvin have been meeting at 5:30 every day to discuss faith and how it works. At the last meeting Rev tells Marvin, "The next time we meet we will go over putting action to your faith." The next day, its lunch time and Marvin sees Leon coming in the cafeteria. Leon sees Marvin and walks over to Marvin's table and sits down. "Yo, what's up Marvin, where you been? It's been almost a month since I heard from you man." Marvin looks up, "hey Leon, what's going on? Man I been reading the Bible, and having bible study with Rev." Leon's surprised, "That's the guy that walks around talking that Jesus stuff all the time right. He's crazy." Marvin defending Rev, "na, he's alright. People just don't understand him." Leon slams his hand on the table and cuts off Marvin, "hold up, let's talk about something that's more important. When are we going to go over are plans for Maryland?" Marvin chewed his food, "we have a couple of years to go over that." "Not me, I go home in a year." Leon hands Marvin an ink pen and paper, "Give me a contact number or something in case I don't see you no more. I just don't want anything to go wrong. I told my people about our plan already." "Oh ok, we are definitely going to hook up. I just need to feed my spirit right now. You know how it is being locked up and all." Leon looks at Marvin with a smirk on his face. "Well you do what you have to do as long as it doesn't interfere with our plans." Leon gets up and leaves the cafeteria, and Marvin went to his room and got his Bible and prayed, then he started reading.

Its 5:15 and Marvin is over at Rev's room already, excited about learning more on how the Bible relates to life. Rev is happy to see Marvin wants to get knowledge on how to live, "Ok, Marvin we're going to move on now that you've learned some about faith and you believe the word of God." Marvin shaking his head up and down, "yeah, yeah of course." "Good, now it's time you learn about listening and doing the word of God and why." "Open your bible to Matthew 7:24-27 it says." Therefore everyone who hears these words of mine and puts them into practice is like a wise man who built his house on the rock. [25] The rain came down, the streams rose, and the winds blew and beat against that house; yet it did not fall, because it had its foundation on the rock. [26] But everyone who hears these words of mine and does not put them into practice is like a foolish man who built his house on sand. [27] The rain came down, the streams rose, and the winds blew and beat against that house, and it fell with a great crash." Rev gave an example, "if you let God direct your path you will have peace, joy, love, and happiness in the time of a storm. And storms are going to come, that's part of life, but you will know how to handle that storm when it comes. Remember, if you let Him, because you have a choice, a choice to do it your way or Gods way. It's really a no brainer. Marvin, you tried it your way before, Rev said throwing his hands up. "Look where it got you."

After studying, Marvin stayed in Revs room, and they talked about the streets for a while, and how easy it is to get caught up with all the temptations. "Rev, I made a lot of money, and I have the opportunity to make more when I get out, but I have a son and girlfriend who I plan on marrying one day, and I can't live a life in and out of jail, running from the cops, worrying about friends setting me up. It's not worth it man." Rev smiling, "well son I am glad to hear you say that, I'm going to tell you like this temptations is like bait on a trap, the devil knows what you like, and he uses it to catch you, it's just like hunting once you put money first the devil baited you in for the kill. You know, there is an order we must follow, God 1st, family 2nd, and finances 3rd, you put God first and 2nd and 3rd will fall in place. Keep that order and watch life come together."

Marvin leaves Revs room happy, he feels like he is finally starting to see things different about life. He is so excited that he goes to his room to write Renee a letter, to tell her God is changing him for the better, and that he wants them to be a family when he comes home. Before he starts to write, he thinks that it would be better if he told her over the phone so he could hear her reaction. It was late and the phones were turned off so he had to wait until the morning.

The next day, Marvin gets up out of bed early to call Renee before she goes to work. He was up reading his Bible most of the night. Seeing the phone is available, he put on his flip flops and runs over to it. Feeling excited while the phone is ringing, but there was no answer and the answering machine came on. Marvin leaving a message, "hey Renee, good morning I thought I could catch you before you left for work, anyway I will call you later. I need to talk to you about something important." After getting no answer from Renee, he goes over to the cafeteria to eat breakfast. Marvin's in a good mood and is walking around speaking to everybody. He can't wait to talk to Renee and tell her his new happiness.

When Marvin walks in the cafeteria he sees Paul, he walks over to the table and sits down with him, "What's up Paul?" Paul pouting, "Nuttin much man, I can't wait to get out of here!" Marvin tries to cheer him up, "hey everyday is a day closer.

Just keep your nose clean and stop gambling." Paul still down and looking sad, "Yeah, but those guys are still messing with me man, calling me broke and stuff, and I had to get a homeboy to pay my debts." Paul shaking his head up and down. "I'll get them back doe, they'll find out who Paul really is." Marvin shaking his head, "do you know who Paul is? "Man just ignore them let them think whatever they want. Do your time and get out of here." Paul looks at Marvin, "who are you man?" "What happen to you, the Marvin I know would be ready to beat those guys down?" "Yeah, well I'm trying to get out of here and do things different. That Marvin you knew is gone, this is the new Marvin, and I have a family that needs me." Paul with a smirk on his face starts laughing, "The new Marvin, say what?" "Are you joking?" With confidence Marvin shakes his head, "yeah, I'm going to get me a 9 to 5, settle down, get married to Renee, and take care of my family." Marvin lifting his hands, I'm no good to them in here." "Man where are you going to find a 9 to 5 making the money that you're use to making? You love the money to much, so stop fooling yourself. You'll be back out there hustling." "Na bro, I believe God is going to make a way and he has a plan for me. My plan didn't work, so I'm going to turn it over to God. Loving money got me in here." Paul laughing, "Oh boy, Rev got you huh?" "I've been seeing you hanging out with him."

After eating and talking they walked outside to get some air. Leon was sitting at the table next to them listening. He watches them as they walked out the cafeteria. Marvin didn't know that Leon was sitting behind him listening. Leon is mad after hearing Marvin tell Paul he is going to stop dealing drugs and get a job. It will mess up his plans. Thinking he is about to lose his Maryland connect, after already making plans, Leon thinks that Rev is becoming a problem. So he figures that he will have to keep Rev away from Marvin. Leon leaves the cafeteria to go look for two guys that he knows named Bruce and Tony. Leon knows them from the street and wants to hire them to keep Rev away from Marvin. Leon knocked on Bruce door, "Yo Bruce, you up? It's me Leon." Bruce, moving slow getting out of the bed, and slipping on his slippers walks over to the door, "hey what's up Leon, what brings you by this morning?" "Man get out of bed and exercise or something, it's almost 9oclock." "I aint got no reason to get up." Bruce is curious about Leon coming to his room, "what's up man?" Getting serious Leon tells

Bruce, "I have a small problem" "What?" "You know that guy they call Rev, he is messing up some plans of mine." "Ok what does that have to do with me?" "I need you and Tony to have a talk with Rev so that he will stay away from that young guy name Marvin." Bruce smiling and rubbing his hands together, "no problem, but it's going to cost you five hundred a piece."

Hours later…

Its noon time, Bruce and Tony are walking around looking for Rev. They went to his room and he wasn't there. They walked outside and saw nothing but rain. They went into the recreation center and there was Rev sitting at a table reading and watching TV. Bruce and Tony walked over to the table and sat down beside Rev, one on the left and the other on his right. Rev looking over the top of his glasses with a smile calmly asked, "Hello gentlemen, how may I help you?" Bruce slams his hand on the table, "Look here man I'm going to get right to the point. We need you to stop hanging around Marvin messing his head up and stuff, and if you don't do it the easy way then we can do it the hard way." Rev with his glasses hanging on his noise and his eyes looking over them, "I'm sorry gentlemen but I can't stop that, it's not up to me." "Well who is it up too?" "See gentleman, this is God's plan not mine, God put this together and He told me to do something so I have to do it no matter what." Tony looking at Rev, and Bruce slams his hand on the table again, "well Rev that's the wrong answer. There are too many people around right now, but we are going to have to take this to another level. You've been warned so don't blame us for what's about to happen to ya, blame God." Rev still calm and humble, "gentleman I am not blaming you all, because ya'll don't know better." Bruce got angry and looked at Tony, "is he calling us stupid?" Tony makes a fist, "what, you calling us stupid, you must want to get beat down right now." Rev puts up his hands, "no…… I'm not saying that at all, what I'm saying is that ya'll don't know that the devil is using ya'll to stop Gods work. See, gentleman me and Marvin meeting and studying the word of God isn't hurting nobody, but the devil. Check this out, he is using ya'll to try and stop God's word from getting to Marvin and ya'll are going to get in trouble and get more jail time for harming me. I will get beat up, so we all lose and the devil is happy. Get it now fellows? In

66

fact, ya'll need to be getting this knowledge as well, so you can know the schemes of the devil." Tony looks at Bruce, "Come on man let's get out of here, the old man is right. We will get more time added on to what we got now, aint no money worth that. I'm trying to get out of here. Tell Leon to do his own dirty work." Bruce and Tony gets up from the table and leave, but Rev heard Tony say, "Tell Leon to do his own dirty work." Rev is wondering who is Leon and why does he wants Marvin to stay away from him.

Its 5:30pm and Marvin met Rev with his bible. Rev puts up his figure, "Before we get started, I have a question to ask you. Does the name Leon sound familiar?" "Yeah, that's this guy I met in here, from New York. Why, what's up?" "I was hoping that it wasn't that Leon. You need to stay away from him, he's up to no good. He doesn't believe and he's out for self-gain. One thing I know about greed is that it's all about self and using people for their own gain. We need to pray for him." Marvin shakes his head up and down. Then they prayed before studying, and they said a special prayer for Leon. "Today we will study about trust, open your Bible to Jeremiah 17: 5- 8. This is what the LORD says, "Cursed is the one who trusts in man, who draws strength from mere flesh and whose heart turns away from the LORD. [6] That person will be like a bush in the wastelands; they will not see prosperity when it comes. They will dwell in the parched places of the desert, in a salt land where no one lives. [7] "But blessed is the one who trusts in the LORD, whose confidence is in him. [8] They will be like a tree planted by the water that sends out its roots by the stream. It does not fear when heat comes; its leaves are always green. It has no worries in a year of drought and never fails to bear fruit." "Meaning don't put your trust in man not even yourself, but blessed is the man that trust in the Lord. Thank you Jesus."

Later on that evening around 7:30, Marvin is hoping Renee is home, so he tries to call her again, and still no answer so he hangs up the phone. While standing at the phone Marvin starts to think about Louis and how is everybody doing so he decides to call his grandparents' house. Grandpop answers the phone, "hello?" Marvin happy to hear Grandpop, "hey Pops how are you?" "I'm fine and what about you how are you making out in there?" "I'm doing good Pop, reading the Bible and learning every day." Marvin hears a child crying in the background, "is that lil Marvin crying, how is my baby boy?" "Yeah that's him Lisa got him over there playing with his toys". Marvin smiling, "ok cool, is Renee there I need to talk to her, I been calling her all day." Grandpop drops his head and was silent for a few seconds. "Ah....Marvin you don't know." "Know what?" Grandpop sadly says, "Marvin, Renee was killed in a car accident two days ago, you didn't know?" Shocked and confused, Marvin is trying to make sure he heard Grandpop correctly. "Renee what, what are you talking about pop?" "No pop no, not Renee. What? No, no, no, no." Marvin crying, "this can't be happening, pop why are you lying to me." Grand pop, not knowing what to say, stays silent. Marvin at disbelief drops the phone, and starts to walk slowly to his room. He can't believe what he just heard. When he gets in his room he looks at Renee pictures, "no man this can't be real." Then it hits him Renee is dead, he starts throwing punches in the air, screaming and crying, hitting the wall. Confused and thinking about his son and Renee, he starts to blame himself. Now his mind is racing feeling guilty and thinking about what could have happened if he was home. The men that are out sitting at the tables watching TV, hears the screaming and crying coming from Marvin's room. Rev and the guys are sitting at a table, and he hears Marvin in his room and walks over to see if everything is ok. When Rev walks in Marvin's room, he's standing in the middle of the floor clinching his teeth and makes a tight fist and is ready to hit Rev. "Rev you better get out of my face right now, I don't need to hear nothing about God right now." Rev puts his hands up in the air, in a surrendering position, and humbling himself. "Son I just came over to check on you, is there anything I can help you with?" Marvin takes his fist and hits the bed and screams at Rev. "Look man, I'm not your son, don't call me that no more, and I thought God was so good huh Rev? Yeah well God took my son's mother away from him, what about that, huh Rev what about that? Renee is dead man, she is dead!" Marvin starts crying again, "God took her away from me." Rev doesn't say a word, he starts walking backwards out of Marvin's room with his hands up in the air, and he went back to the table and sat down. Telling the other guys what happen, "hey guys we need to pray for Marvin, his son's mother was killed in a car accident." The men held hands and prayed. Later that night Marvin finally cried himself to sleep.

The next day he wakes up hoping that yesterday was a bad dream. He starts to think about Renee again, his mind is at war right now, he is confused and don't know what to do. Upset Marvin starts thinking it's a waste of time trying to do right reading the Bible. Lying in bed staring at the ceiling shaking his head, Marvin decides to give up on trying to do good. Later that afternoon, Marvin is still in the bed thinking about Renee, then he gets angry and he wants to take it out on somebody. Not caring anymore he gets out of bed. Feeling he lost everything he walks out his room mad. Then he walks outside, while walking around the yard he sees Paul and approaches him, "what's up man?" Paul can see that Marvin had been crying, and that something is wrong, "nothin, just waiting for the next basketball game." Marvin's looking for a fight. "Hey man, those guys still bothering you?" "Yeah they can have their laugh for now, but I'll get the last laugh later." Marvin looking around, "I tell you what if you know where they are we can go handle them right now." Paul gets excited, "for real?" "Yeah man lets go find em." "Let's go, that's what I'm talking about, that's the Marvin I know." Marvin and Paul started walking around looking for these guys that keep picking with Paul, they walked around the yard, the gym, and then they went inside the building. Paul shouting, "where yall at." Everybody sees Marvin and Paul walking around and everyone can tell that something is about to go down, because of the way Paul is acting.

Now the word had gotten out that Marvin and Paul are looking for these guys. Paul sees one of them playing pool, "hey there is one of them right there." They started walking towards him. Rev heard about what was going on and sees Marvin walking towards the pool table. Rev walks over and grabbed Marvin by the arm, Marvin swung a punch at Rev, Rev leans back, and Marvin missed, Rev grabbed him, "Look Marvin, I'm not getting in your business, but I have one thing to say." "You have a three year old son to think about, and your son needs you out there not in here, if you go and get yourself in more trouble that means more time or who knows you might not ever get out here, then your son will be alone in this world. It's not fair to him man." Rev let Marvin go and walked away, "that's all I have to say."

Paul is standing still looking and waiting for Marvin to catch up with him, "come on man." Marvin looking at the floor thinking about what Rev said about his son, and then he hits the wall, undecided for a minute about what to do he turns around and goes to his room.

Marvin stayed in bed for two days, later that evening he realizes that he needs to talk to a counselor about going to Renee funeral he jumps up out of bed and gets dressed. He tells the guard that he needs a furlough request form for a funeral and the guard gets him a form to fill out. On the form it asks for the date of the funeral, so he calls grandma's house to get the date and Lisa answers the phone. "Hey Marvin, how are you?" "Hey Lisa, I'm glad I caught you." Lisa is curious. "Why are you so glad you caught me?" "Because, I need the date of the funeral so I can come home for the funeral." Lisa not sure, "it's Friday." Marvin hears nothing in the background while Lisa is talking, "Where is little Marvin. It's quiet. Where is everybody?" Lisa shaking her head, "Marvin Renee's parents came and got little Marvin, they said that they don't want him here around a bunch of drug dealers and gangbangers." "They said what? They are trying to take my boy from me, are they crazy? Nahhhh man I need to get out of here. I can't take it no more."

Marvin thanks Lisa and hangs up the phone. He completed the furlough form for the funeral and took it over to the guard. The guard goes over the form with Marvin, "hey you didn't fill out this part here about how long you and your wife were married." "We weren't married she was my girlfriend, and we have a son together." "Sorry but furloughs are only used for spouses, parents, children, and sometimes siblings, sorry about that." Marvin walks away angry about not being able to go to Renee's funeral and now he's thinking about Renee's parents trying to take little Marvin away from him. He starts walking around the dorm confused talking to himself. One minute he blames his self because he thinks that things would have been different if he was home. Still walking around the dorm wondering what can he do, he passes Rev's room and see the guys in there fellowshipping. Marvin shakes his head thinking those guy are wasting their time, and keeps walking. The more he walks the more he thinks about everything that is going on, then he realizes, there is nothing he can do, So he goes to his room and tries to calm down and get his mind on something different. But he can't stop thinking about Renee, her parents, and his son. He grabs his head and screams, "Ahhhhhh." Crying and feeling this is the worst day of his life, and he can't take no more. He can't find answers to his questions, so now he is thinking what does he have to live for.

Meanwhile, Rev and the other guys are in Rev's room sharing testimonies and talking about their struggles, and how God brought them through. Rev opens his Bible and starts to read a scripture to the men. When he finished reading, he looks up and sees Marvin standing at the doorway with his Bible with tears coming down his face, "I have nowhere else to go." "Please help me." Rev stood up with his arms open, "If you want help, you have come to the right place." The other men stood up and welcome Marvin in the room, some had been through what Marvin is going through. They can see the tears in Marvin's eyes, they all gave him a brotherly hug. After receiving Marvin with open arms, Rev smiles, "Son you need peace, it's time you learn about JESUS!"

Two years later.

Rev and Marvin spent the last two year reading about Jesus. Today is Marvin's last day at the prison, he goes home tomorrow. He spends his last day taking pictures off the wall and going through letters to see which ones to save and throw away. Its right before dinner time and Marvin walks over to Rev's room to talk to him. Rev's in his room folding clothes when Marvin walks in. "Well, Rev this is it, my last day man. I'm going home tomorrow." Happy to see how much Marvin has matured in the Word, Rev gives him advice, "Yeah, you go home and be patient and do it Gods way. Remember, His plan is the best plan. It might not come when you want it, but God knows when the time is right." Marvin sticks out his hand for a hand shake, "That's right, God plan is the best plan, but I would like to thank you for everything. I wouldn't have made it without you man." Rev is pointing his figure up in the air, "All glory to God. He made this possible so thank Him. Now I'm going to tell you, your real test is out there, remember you will pass the test every time no matter how hard the test gets, as long as you put God first. Now go get something to eat, this is your last meal here. Marvin laughing, "Yeah ok the food is great." Marvin looking at Rev with a curious look on his face, he wants to ask Rev a question, and Rev sees that Marvin has something to say, "Is it something on your mind Marvin?" Marvin hesitates, "Since you asked, I never heard you talk about why you are here, and how much time you have. I know that it is none of my business, but I am going home tomorrow and I was just wondering." With a grin on his face, Rev starts talking, "Well I believe it is part of Gods plan, He sent me here to save souls by giving people His instruction on life. And I don't really talk about how I got here, because that part of my life is behind me and I like to look forward, but if someone asks, I don't mind telling them. So what happened is that I had a cousin ask me for a ride to the convenience store to cash his check." Rev thinking back, "I had just brought a new car, and man it was nice, but anyway he asked me to take him because he needed some cash to pay a bill. So when we got to the store, we walked inside. I went to go get a soda, and my cousin went to go get some money. There was only one problem, he didn't have a check, but he had a gun. I heard the gun go off so I ran over to see what happened. The cashier was lying on the floor and my cousin was gone. He left running and I got scared and ran to my car. When I pulled off, the police cars came from every direction and surrounded me and the rest is history." Marvin was listening with a plain look on his face, "Wow, what ever happened to your cousin?" "Oh he's married and raising a family, and have a good job the last I heard." Marvin shaking his head, "I don't know Rev. I think that I would be mad with your cousin." Rev still smiling, "Oh I was very upset and hurt. Look Marvin, I spent 4 years fighting my case, and 6 years thinking about revenge. Those 6 years was killing me. I couldn't do nothing but think about getting my cousin back. He had control of my life 24 hours a day for 6 years. But when I found Jesus, I found forgiveness and peace and got my life back. I forgave my cousin, forgiveness set me free and it will set you free. I'm here doing life and working for God hoping to save souls, and whatever His plans are for me, let His will be done. I turned it all over." Marvin got the answer that he had been waiting to hear. They both left the room headed to the cafeteria for chow. Sitting down eating, Marvin watches Rev standing in line tapping a new inmate on the shoulder. He sees Rev introducing himself to the man. Marvin smiled. It reminded him of the day Rev tapped him on the shoulder changing his life.

Turning around from the table, Marvin sees Paul standing behind him. Paul, trying to look happy for Marvin, "congratulations, so you going home tomorrow. Tell the boys I'll see them in five years." Marvin surprised, "five years, I thought we were going home around the same time." Paul shaking his head, "na, I got caught up in some stuff, and they gave me five more years." Marvin wants to walk away from Paul, making short conversation, "man stay away from trouble, hey I got to go talk to you later." Marvin starts to walk away fast, he know Paul is up to something, Paul is shouting "Marvin hold up, hold up I need a favor." Marvin kept walking as if he didn't hear Paul. Paul had plans to ask Marvin to go borrow money and snacks from people that didn't know he is going home tomorrow, and give everything to him. Marvin is going home tomorrow, thinking about Louis running wild, Renee's parents wanting nothing to do with him, and lil Marvin and having to start all over. This is where everything begins.

Meanwhile back at home church service had just ended, and Pastor Tim gave a message on forgiveness, reading from Matthew 6:14-15, [14] for if you forgive other people when they sin against you, your heavenly Father will also forgive you. [15] But if you do not forgive others their sins, your Father will not forgive your sins. And Robin sang songs of praise and worship that had everybody uplifted and praising.

Church service just ended and everyone is leaving except Pastor Tim. He went back to his office and closed the door and dropped to his knees thanking God for his six year anniversary of being free from alcohol. On his knees with his hands lifted up and looking up to the ceiling with tears in his eyes he shouts, "Thank You Lord, thank You." Wiping the tears from his eyes, he remembers how he lost his wife and son because of his alcohol battle. Then he gets up and cleans his face and looks around for his briefcase and car keys. Glancing at the clock, he grabs them both and leaves the church. Pastor Tim is on his way to Grandma's house for Sunday's dinner. Grandma still loves to cook dinner every Sunday for family and friends. While driving Pastor Tim calls his ex-wife Ericka, he hears someone answer the phone but no one says anything, "hello, hello, anybody there?" "Yes Tim?" "Hello….. I was just calling to see how you and Steven are doing." "We're fine, we just got home from church." "Speaking of church, when are y'all going to come visit my church?" Then there is silence again. Ericka wants to say yes because see still loves Tim, but she remembers the fights and different women when he was drinking. "Would that be a good idea Tim?" "Of course, I can't think of a better place to see my wife and son." Then there is silence again and Pastor Tim speaks up, "hey you know today is my six year anniversary being clean from alcohol." Ericka is happy to hear that, "It is? Has it been that long? Congratulations! I will keep praying for you. I have to go now Tim, it's getting late." "Oh ok, talk to you later and tell Steven his dad said hi for me."

Pastor Tim pulls up in front of grandma's house and he can't find a place to park. Having to park several houses away and thinking that he might be late, he walks down the sidewalk at a fast pace and runs up the steps and walks inside the house without knocking. Feeling relieved to see that he wasn't late, he speaks to everybody and walks into the living room where Lisa was sitting on the couch watching TV, "Hey Lisa how you and the kids doing?" "Everybody's fine." "Does Mike help you with the kids?" Lisa looks at Pastor Tim with her eyes open wide, and shakes her head "no, he can't even help his self, besides he is someone else's problem now." Louis walks in, "hey Pastor Tim, what's up?" Pastor Tim looks up at Louis, "nothing much Louis, how are you? I haven't seen you at church lately." Changing the subject smiling and excited, Louis tells Pastor Tim while rubbing his hands together, "I'm good, but hey my big cuz Marvin is coming home tomorrow."

Pastor Tim looks surprise, "Oh good, glad to hear that, you know he wrote me a few times. He had some questions about the Bible, and I had sent him some reading materials. I hope that it helped him and that he will continue to seek the Lord." Louis' wondering why Marvin has questions about the Bible, "We been going to church sense we were little he should know the Bible by now Pastor." Pastor Tim tries to explain to Louis. "Louis, it's more to it than just going to church, you need to know how to read the Bible." "Well I know Marvin and he is going to seek money, no disrespect Pastor but this is what Marvin needs." Louis pulled out a lot of cash out his pocket, "when he come home this is all he need, I mean come on everybody needs money to make it, right?" Before Pastor Tim could answer Louis, Grandma called everybody to come and eat dinner, Louis jumps up, "hold that thought Pastor Tim, it's time to eat, later."

Everybody made their way to the dining room table. Everyone is standing around the table while Pastor Tim blesses the food. Louis is looking around the table at the food hoping that Pastor Tim would hurry up. Afterwards everyone started digging. There was a knock at the door. Louis goes to answer the door and it was Kevin, Kim, and their kids. Kevin walks in happy to see that they had just started eating, "sorry we're late, I had to send some emails for work." Grandpop worried about Kevin, "what I tell you about working yourself to death? You need a break from work, plus I don't see my grandkids anymore. You need a vacation. Kim looks at Kevin, "yeah when are we going to take a vacation?" Kevin started eating and stuffing his mouth so he wouldn't have to answer Kim or Grandpop.

After dinner everybody was stuffed and moving slow. Thanking Grandma for a delicious dinner, Kim and Lisa helped Grandma clean the kitchen, and the men went outside on the porch. Lisa left Grandma and Kim in the kitchen and waited until her and Grandpop was alone so she could ask him to watch her kids while she goes to the movies with a new boyfriend named Rick. She knew Grandma would say no. After everything was cleaned up and put away, Grandma and Kim came outside to join the men on the porch, and Lisa was getting dressed for her date to go to the movies. Everybody is on the porch talking about Marvin coming home tomorrow, and no one has seen little Marvin in 3 years. Kevin and Kim are getting ready to leave, because Kevin wants to go home and get ready for work.

Then a strange car with dark tinted windows pulls up and parks, and blows the horn. Everyone is looking at the car waiting for someone to get out, but no one gets out. Louis gets paranoid, he doesn't trust anyone. Finally, Lisa comes running out on the porch shouting, and walking fast to the car "hey that's my ride. I got to go. I see you all later." Grandma, wondering where is Lisa going, "where do you think you're going without your kid's young lady." Lisa walking fast, "I'm going to the movies with my new friend, I'll be back and Grandpop said he'll watch the kids for me." Grandma looks at Grandpop, "she got you again. I told you she needs to be more responsible with those kids, and you need to stop doing that." Kevin and Louis are upset about the way Lisa's friend pulled up and didn't introduce himself to Grandma and Grandpop. Kevin yells at Lisa, "your new friend can't get out the car and introduce himself to my parents? Tell him it's rude to pull up to someone's house and just blow the horn and don't speak." Lisa, ignoring Kevin and Louis, gets in the car and closes the door then they pulled off. She gives Rick a kiss and he doesn't kiss her back. Lisa feels that something is wrong, "ok what's wrong baby?" Frustrated Rick tells Lisa. "Baby I'm tired of having to borrow my cousin's car, and having to pick you up from your grandma's house." Lisa's not thinking that it's not a big deal. "It's ok, things will get better for us, just be patient." "But Lisa we been dating for four months now, and I uhh, you know, I got feelings for you, ok. I love you and I want us to live together and be a family so our kids can play together and you know do the family thing." Lisa's excited and smiling, "did you say you love me and want to be a family?" Rick's shaking his head yes. Lisa asked, "Are you ready for something like that?" "Because I want the same thing, to be a family, and I love you too boo. You know Rick, we can start saving our money to get a place and car." Rick cuts her off. "Save up, baby you can, I'm still looking for a job but I know another way. My cousin's girlfriend has two kids and the state got her a place and a car for lil nothing. Baby you can do the same thing and we can be together." "Ok, ok I'll check on it ok. Let's enjoy the movie for now and have a nice time."

Meanwhile, everybody had left Grandma's house and went their separate ways. Kevin and Kim went straight home. On the way home, Kevin starts talking about work and getting a supervisor position. "Ok Kim, help me out here, what you think about me applying for a supervisor's position at work." Kim tries to speak but Kevin keeps talking over her trying to convince her. "Now you know we could use the money, plus think about it, I'll be supervisor and that's always been my goal." Still trying to get a word in Kim just started talking. "Honey, all I have to say is pray about it, and ask God what he wants you to do." Kevin looks at Kim. "Well baby, I already applied and I have a good chance of getting the position. I'll know this week. They normally send an email out before they talk to you in person, but I thought I let you know." Kim is staring at Kevin, not saying a word. When they got home, Kim gets the kids ready for the family movie before bed time while Kevin checks his email again. Kim and the kids are wondering where Kevin is, then they hear a shout from the bedroom. Kevin is shouting, "thank you Lord, thank you, thank you." Kim gets up and goes see what is going on and the kids ran behind her, "Kevin, what's going on?" "What happened?" Kevin shouts, "I got the job, I got the job I'm a supervisor now! Here look at this, read this baby. Kim reads the email, "Kevin, this job is at night and you must be available on weekends. When are you going to have time for church and your family? Kevin, I don't know." Kevin, trying to convince Kim, "but baby it's an extra 10,000 dollars a year and I always wanted to be a supervisor. I'm getting older not younger." The kids hear Kevin and Kim talking about the schedule of his new position and their oldest son, Jr. is thinking that his dad isn't going to be around no more and feels alone. Kim leaves out the bedroom and takes the kids back in the living room. While walking to the living room Jr. asks Kim, "Mom, does this mean we're never going to see daddy anymore?" Kim shakes her head, "no it doesn't mean that Jr. Your daddy will still be here, he will just work different hours."

Meanwhile Pastor Tim was over a sick church member's house named Mr. Smith. Pastor Tim tries to visit Mr. Smith at least once a week. While Pastor Tim and Mr. Smith were in the living room talking, there was a knock at the door. Mr. Smith, not able to get around much asked Pastor Tim, "can you get that for me Pastor?" "Sure, you sit right there I got it." Pastor Tim jumps up and walks down the hall. Opening the door, he sees a very attractive woman standing there. Curious and thinking to himself," who is this beautiful woman?" She smiles and sticks out her hand, "hello my name is Tina, is my father home?" Pastor Tim, still staring, pauses for a second, "yes, yes please come in, and is Mr. Smith your father? "Yes he is." "Ok, well we were just sitting here talking." Pastor Tim holds the door for Tina as she walks in and smells a very nice fragrance. He is at a loss of words while walking behind Tina down the hall. Pastor Tim introduces himself to Tina. "I'm the Pastor at you fathers church, I just came by to check on him and to see if there is anything that I could do to help out." Tina laughing, "I'm sure he appreciates that. Thanks for checking on him." Tina sees father, "Hey dad, how are you? She gives her father a kiss on the cheek, and sits on the arm of the chair beside him. "I see you have company." Mr. Smith stands up, "I'm feeling much better Tina, and this is my Pastor. Pastor this is my baby girl Tina. She stops by and checks on me often since my wife passed." Mr. Smith looks around and asked Tina, "Where's John?" "Oh you know John, he's with the guys. Its football season so he spends his time at the sports bars with the guys this time of the year." Laughing and shaking her head, Tina says, "come to think of it, I don't see him during basketball, and baseball season neither." Pastor Tim grabs his keys, "well it's time for me to go. I'm going to get out you all's way." Tina looks at Pastor Tim, "no please don't leave. Dad is enjoying your company." Walking towards the door, Pastor Tim tells Tina, "I just came by to check on your dad and pray with him. So I'm going to move on now but I have two more stops to make." Pastor Tim waves his hand while glancing at Tina, "I'll see you later Mr. Smith and nice meeting you Tina." Tina smiling, "My pleasure." Mr. Smith waving his hand "ok Pastor Tim, thanks for coming by and tell everyone that I will be back soon." Tina walks Pastor Tim to the door, "thank you for visiting my father, it really helps him." "No problem at all, I really enjoy it." Soon after Pastor Tim leaves, Tina walks back in the room with her father and asks him, "is the Pastor married? He's a nice looking man." Mr. Smith looks at Tina, "no he's not, but you sure are, so why you asking?" Tina grins, "There is no harm in asking a question."

Later that evening Pastor Tim just got home, he lays his briefcase and keys on the table and gets ready to relax and watch TV. He checks his phone messages first and he's surprised to see that there is only one message. It was from the church choir lead singer Robin, asking Pastor Tim for a one on one meeting tomorrow. Because of the tone in her voice, Pastor Tim is wondering if everything was ok. So he makes a note to call Robin in the morning.

Meanwhile, Louis had gone over to Troy's apartment to watch the football games. Scoota and Fat Frank were already there. And Troy called his girlfriend and invited her and two of her friends over. Troy had just moved in his new apartment on the fifth floor in a high rise building with new furniture and a new sixty inch TV. Troy had two buckets of fried chicken on the dining room table and the refrigerator full of sodas and alcohol. Troy, Louis, and Fat Frank are on the balcony talking and Scooter is on the couch flipping the channels from one game to another when he hears a knock at the door. Scooter shouts "yo, Troy, somebody's knocking at your door." Troy yells back through the balcony door, "Get it for me, its Tanya and them." Louis, Fat Frank, and Scoota are wondering how the girls look, because they never met Tanya. All they know about her is that Troy has feelings for her and doesn't bring her around when he's with his crew. Scooter opens the door and the girls walked in. Troy comes in the apartment and Louis looks at Fat Frank, "man you see that?" "Yeahhh, I think it's time to go watch the game." "I agree." Then Louis and Fat Frank went back into the apartment. Troy introduces the guys to Tanya and her girlfriends. Louis is standing in the middle of the floor holding a cup in one hand and sticks out the other hand to Tanya and her friends, "what's up ladies?" Louis starts showing off right away, "we should go to my place. I have much more space, a theater, and a pool table." Everybody said no, they were comfortable at the Troy's apartment. An hour went by and everybody is watching the game, laughing and joking having a good time, but Louis started to act like he was better than his crew telling Tanya and her friends, "yeahhhh if it wasn't for me these jokers wouldn't have nothing." Louis notices that the girls were giving Troy, Scoota, and Fat Frank more attention than him. Now he starts to brag about how much money he has and what he's going to get. Louis is acting like a real loud showoff in front of the girls. Tanya is getting tired of hearing Louis' mouth and changes the subject, "Troy, I love your furniture, you got a nice place here." Before Troy could answer Louis cuts him off, "he wouldn't have any of this if it wasn't for me." Troy, Scooter and Fat Frank are looking at each other like what is Louis doing, they definitely don't like the way he's acting. They started to feel disrespected. Tanya and her friends are tired of Louis and want to leave. Tanya stands up and wave her hand to her girlfriends, "Troy, it's time for us to go, call me when you are by yourself." Louis got up and went to the bathroom, and Troy, Scooter, and Fat Frank are talking among each other about how wrong Louis was acting. Louis comes back and sits down, so Troy changed the subject and walked Tanya and her friends to the door. The guys were very angry with Louis but they didn't show it. They acted like everything was ok.

An hour went by and it was getting late so Louis tells Troy, "look, man I got to go. I have to drive three hours to pick up Marvin tomorrow from lock up." Troy angry, "Yeah you better go get you some sleep man." Troy walks Louis to the door, then they give each other a fist pound and shoulder bump, "later." Troy walks back in the living room shaking his head at disbelief, "I already know what ya'll going say, it's messed up what he did." Scooter looks at Troy, "yeah we're supposed to be family, not his workers. What up with that?" Fat Frank shakes his head, "yeah man, and in front of your girl." So the guys watched the rest of the games and talked about Louis the rest of the night.

The next day.

It's Monday morning and Lisa is at work and Rick calls her cell phone to remind her to call social services about getting a place and money for a car. Lisa at work sitting at her desk sees the caller ID and answers the phone whispering, "heyyyy baby, how are you?" "I'm good." "Did you enjoy the movie last night?" "Yeah it was alright. Hey did you call social services yet?" "No I'm at work and I don't need these people all up in my business. I'll do it when I get off work." Sounding disappointed Rick tells her, "You need to stop worrying about what people think. We need a place to live. You can call when you go to lunch or something. They might be closed when you get off work." "Ok, ok, I'll see what I can do, and I'll call you back. I have to go, call you later."

Meanwhile at Kevin's job, he's in orientation for his new position. He found out his new schedule and responsibilities for the supervisor position and he knows Kim isn't going to like it. After orientation, a co-worker walks over to Kevin,

"Congrats Kevin, you deserve it. I would have applied but my kids are keeping me busy right now, and I can't work night shift." Kevin listening and thinking about Kim and the Kids, he grins, "Yeah it's Sunday thru Thursday 9pm-5am, but sometimes you have to sacrifice things to get what you want, besides my family understands and they're happy for me." His co-worker shakes his hand, "good, I'm happy to hear that." "Thanks."

At the church Pastor Tim is in his office and calls Robin to see what she wants to meet about. Robin answers her phone, "hello." "Praise the Lord, Robin I got your message? Would you like to meet today?" Robin at work, "yes Tim, I will be by your office around 4." Pastor Tim hears her tone and is really curious now, "sounds good I'll be here, but is everything ok?" "I don't want to talk on the phone. I rather talk to you in person. I'll be by around 4 and we'll talk then." Pastor Tim confused "ok Robin, I'll be here." He hangs up the phone wondering what's wrong and sits back in his chair thinking.

Meanwhile at the prison, it's time for Marvin to be released. Louis is waiting out front of the prison. He's been waiting for two hours already. Marvin finally comes walking out, looking around he sees freedom, takes a deep breath and walks down the sidewalk. Louis is sitting in his truck sees Marvin walking. Excited about seeing his cousin, he blows the horn. Marvin turns around and looks in the parking lot and sees an all-black new Cadillac Escalade. Because the windows were darkened with tint, Marvin couldn't see inside. Then Louis jumps out the truck. Marvin sees Louis dressed in an all-white sweat suit with red and blue trimming, wearing a white gold chain hanging down to his stomach with diamonds and a matching watch and ring. Louis meets Marvin half way, and they hug, "what's up cuzzo, happy to see ya home." "Yeah I'm home, home for good man, I'm never going back in that place." Marvin turns around and looks at the prison. Louis opens the door for Marvin, "come on let's get out of here, let's go see the fam."

While driving down the highway, Louis notice Marvin isn't saying much. "Hey cuz you got a lot of catching up to do, but don't worry about business everything is good. I'm pulling in sixty g's a week now and got Troy and 'em working." Marvin looks at Louis, "man I'm done with that life. I'm going to get a 9 to 5 and raise my son." "You going to do what, man what you talking about? Who's going to hire you? You just getting out the joint." "Yeah I know, I just got to be patient. I know it's going to be hard in the beginning but I can do it." Then Marvin changes the subject, "but anyway take me to see grandma first, and then I want to go by Renee's parents house to see lil Marvin, we can talk about money later."

Meanwhile its noon time and Lisa is on lunch break, so she calls Rick. "Yooooo." "Hello, I got some good news for you, I was approved for a place and all I have to do is go fill out the application." "What, tell your job you have an emergency and you have to go." "I don't know they be tripping around here, I'll see what I can do."

The day went by and its 4:00 and Robin is at the church to meet with Pastor Tim. Pastor Tim is sitting at his desk while still feeling curious about what Robin wants to talk to him about. He looks at the clock and hears a knock at the door. "Yes, come in." Robin walks in and sits down. "Hello Robin, how are you? Before we start lets pray first." After praying Pastor Tim tells Robin, "just would like to say Robin what a nice job you have done with the choir and the musicians. You have done a really great job, and I pray that everything is ok." "Thank you Pastor, well that's what I want to talk to you about so I'm going to get right to the point. Since I've been here, I brought up the choir and the music and I feel I'm worth more than $200 a Sunday." Pastor Tim is relieved because he now knows what Robin wants now. "It's true, God has truly given you a gift, but the church can barely afford the $200 you get now." "Well I'm going to be honest with you Tim, I'm the reason people come to this church. All you hear is them talking about how good the music sounds and they love my singing." Then Robin goes in her purse and pulls out a card and shows it to Pastor Tim. "Tim I was offered three hundred dollars a show to sing with an R&B group, and there could be five to seven shows a week and if the church can't give me more money then I'm gone. "Well Robin pray about it, should you be using your gift for a club?" "I don't need to pray about it, I'm going with the money. I have to look out for Robin 'cause nobody else is." Pastor Tim is disappointed, "well if that's how you feel I wish you well and I will be praying for you. But remember God gave you this gift for his glory." Robin being sarcastic, "I think God understands." Then she walks out.

Meanwhile at Kevin's job the orientation is over, and he's heading home, thinking about how he is going to tell Kim about his new schedule. Kevin pulls up in his driveway feeling anxiety, cause he doesn't know how Kim is going to react. Kevin walked in the house shouting, "hey where is everybody?" The kids came running and hugged Kevin, then Kim comes in walking slowly with her arms folded, "ok Kevin, how did it go?" Kevin hesitates, "well I got the job duties and schedule." Kim looks at Kevin, "ok let's hear it, hope it's not too bad." "Well it's Sunday through Thursday from 9pm-5am." "Now Kevin you know that's not going to work. We will never see you, and what about the kid's activities? And if you work on Sundays you'll miss church. This is not going to work for us right now." Kevin cuts off Kim, "just let me at least try it out and see what happens." Jr. is listening to the conversation and feels sad about his father's new schedule. Thinking he won't see his father much, he gets angry and goes to his room and lies in his bed and stares at the ceiling.

Meanwhile at Troy's apartment, Scooter and Fat Frank are still angry about the way Louis treated them yesterday. Sitting around talking, they all agreed on getting Louis back. Scooter shakes his head, "yo lets set him up to get busted." Troy looks at Scooter, "Na man, we all will get busted, besides we aint snitching on nobody." Fat Frank looks up rubbing his hand together, "let's take what he loves most, his money and stash." They all agreed with Fat Frank, "that's what's up". Taking his money and stash would hurt him the most. So that no one gets hurt they decided to break in his house when he's not home. Then Troy speaks up, "yeah, I'll hang out with him to find out where he keeps everything." Fat Frank still rubbing his hands together, "ok then, let's do it."

At grandma's house, Louis and Marvin are finished visiting. Marvin tells Louis, "Ok I'm ready to see little Marvin man. He makes his visit with little Marvin his last stop so he could spend some time with him. Pulling up in front of Renee parent's house Marvin feels excited, nervous, and anxiety because he doesn't know what to expect. Marvin sees both cars parked in the driveway, so he believes that they're home. Marvin gets out the car and runs to the door. Marvin knocks on the door, and there is no answer, so he knocks again and still, no answer. Knocking and knocking on the door, he hears something move so he knocks again and again no answer. After five minutes of knocking on the door, Marvin walks back to the truck and decides to leave and try later. As Louis is driving, he's talking to Marvin about how business is going and Marvin puts his hand up. "Louis I'm going to tell you some good stuff, this drug business is a dead end. You are going to wind up in jail or dead. It's just a matter of time. The five years of my life in prison was not fun, but I believe God put me there to slow me down and save my life! It's by the grace of God I'm not dead now, you know about Travis's crew." Louis glances at Marvin and turns forward, "oh, you gettin religious on me now. What about this money out here? How can you give that up, besides I keep telling you, aint nobody hiring. You'll be back in the game. Watch, it's just a matter of time cuz. You talking religious now because you just got out. Give it a while, you'll see." Marvin shaking his head, "na, you don't get it do you, I'm not going back. I believe God is going to make a way for me." "Man I hear what you saying, you act like I don't go to church. Ok I tell you what, asks God to give me some money and I'll stop dealing," Louis, joking starts laughing.

Meanwhile at Mr. Smith's house, Pastor Tim goes to visit Mr. Smith. When he pulls up he sees Tina's car, and he start thinking about how attractive she is. He quickly reminds himself that she's married, so he stays focused on his visit with Mr. Smith. Pastor Tim knocks at the door. Tina answers and invites him in the house. "Hello Pastor Tim, how are you?" "I am doing well, and yourself?" "I'm ok, sitting here watching TV by myself." "By yourself, where's your dad?" "Is he ok?" "Yes he's well, he's actually doing better. He just kept falling asleep with the TV watching him (giggling) so I made him go lay down." "Ok, glad to hear that he is doing better. Well please tell him I came by to check on him and I will catch up with him later." Tina wants to continue conversation so she invites him to stay. "If you don't have any more visits to make, I just made some coffee,, would you like some?" "No thanks I better get going." Then he thinks about his day and meeting with Renee know and sees nothing wrong with a cup of coffee. "You know what, I did have a crazy day today. I guess I could use a cup, thanks." Pastor Tim sits down in the living room with his hands patting his knees, while Tina is making him a cup of coffee. Tina comes in the room with Pastor Tim's cup of coffee. She hands it to him and she has hers. Tina gets comfortable kicking off her shoes and sits down with her feet on the couch. She gives Pastor Tim the remote control to the TV, "find something to watch." Pastor Tim turning the channels, then Tina asks, "Where did you go to school?" Telling Tina what school he went to and the neighborhood that he grew up in, they both found out that they knew some of the same people and that they might have crossed paths because they use to hang out at the same places. Enjoying his conversation Pastor Tim asked Tina, "could I have another cup of coffee."

Meanwhile on the street everybody is talking about Marvin being home and looking for revenge against Bobby. Bobby hears about the rumor on the street that Marvin is looking for him to get revenge. Thinking that Marvin is after him, Bobby keeps his gun on him all the time now. Now Bobby is telling everybody that he is going to get Marvin before he gets him.

A week later, everyone is moving forward with their plans. Lisa and her boyfriend moved into her new apartment and got a nice used van. Marvin is still job hunting every day, but because of his background he keeps getting turned down. Kevin started his new supervisor position at night and working weekends. He doesn't have time for his family or church and Jr. is angry and starts to hang with the wrong crowd. Louis is still riding around showing off and Troy is hanging with him to find out where he keeps his money.

Robin started rehearsals with her new band, and Pastor Tim stopped going to Mr. Smith house because of the temptation he felt when he and Tina had their conversation last week. He felt the attraction between them and thought it would be best that he stayed away from her. He hasn't seen Mr. Smith in six days now.

It's Sunday morning and everyone is in church except Kevin, he is at home resting for work tonight. The choir was singing without Robin, and Pastor Tim was in his office getting the sermon ready. Ten minutes into the choir singing, a woman walks in the church and sits down in the back of the church. It's hard to see her face because of the hat she is wearing, and she is wearing a body fitted dress that has men turning heads. Pastor Tim comes out his office and starts the church service. After singing another song, Pastor Tim stands up at the pulpit. He felt that he needs to speak on temptation. "Turn your Bible to

1 Corinthians 10:12, it says," [12] So if you think you are standing <u>firm</u>, be careful that you don't fall! [13] No temptation has overtaken you except what is common to mankind. And God is faithful; he will not let you be tempted beyond what you can bear. But when you are tempted, he will also provide a way out so that you can endure it.

At the end of the service Pastor Tim asked, "If there are any visitors that would like to stand and introduce themselves, they may do so at this time." The woman seated in the back stood up, "Hello everyone my name is Tina, I'm Mr. Smith daughter, and he would like for y'all to know that he is well and will be returning soon." The congregation started rejoicing and clapping about the good news that Mr. Smith is doing well. Pastor Tim stood silent for a moment staring at Tina and then he started clapping still staring at Tina and she was staring back at him. He was surprised and happy, but scared because he was happy to see her. While everyone was leaving church, Pastor Tim went to his office and sat down. Wondering what Tina was doing here, he hears someone walking down the hall, then a knock on the door. Pastor Tim sitting is at his desk with his hand over his face, he knew it was Tina, and then another knock.

Pastor Tim wants to see her, but knows he shouldn't, and then he shouts, "Come in." The door opens and it was Tina. Tina walks in smiling, "Hello Pastor, how are you?" "That was a good word today." "I am fine Tina, I can't complain. God is good." "Well I thought I ask because we haven't heard from you in a week, you know. I was looking forward to you coming by my father's house to drink coffee and chat some."

Pastor Tim, thinking that he needs to tell Tina that he had to stop coming over her father's house because of her, takes a deep breath, "Tina, um I going to be honest with you." Tina nods her head ok. "I had to stop coming around you because I'm attracted to you and you're everything I'm looking for in a woman, but you are married and I'm working on getting my family back and I'm a man of God. So I have to stay away." Now that Tina knows that Pastor Tim is attracted to her, she walks closer to him, "what's wrong with that?" Then she kisses him, Pastor Tim is kissing back for a minute and then he pushes her back and looks at her and started kissing her again for another minute and pushed her back again. "No I can't do this Tina, please you have to go." "Do you want me to leave?" Tina asked smiling. "No, I mean yes. No I don't want you to go, but you have to." Tina puts her finger over Pastor Tim's mouth while he was still talking, "Ok, I'll leave; but if you change your mind and like some coffee, I'll be at my father's house tomorrow around six. Bye." Tina leaves and Pastor Tim sits down, feeling convicted and asking for forgiveness for kissing Tina.

Marvin is out front of the church waiting for Pastor Tim to give him a ride to grandma's house. While waiting, Marvin is telling the teenagers about how the streets are trouble and to stay in school. Jr. was standing with the group of teens, and Kim walks over to Marvin, "it's hard taking care of the kids with Kevin working at night and weekends, Jr. is really missing him." After talking to Kim, Marvin walks back into the church to see what is taking Pastor Tim such a long time to come out the church. Walking down the hall Marvin hears some talking. As he gets closer to Pastor Tim's office, he realizes its Pastor Tim asking for forgiveness for kissing Tina. Marvin stops walking and turns around, and runs back outside and catches a ride with Kim and Jr.

At Grandma's house, no one showed up but Louis and Marvin. Kim had to go home to get the kids ready for school tomorrow and tries to see Kevin before he goes to work. Pastor Tim went home just to find him making excuses and reasons why he should go by Mr. Smith house tomorrow. Lisa didn't go to church or Grandma's house. She cooked food at her apartment for Rick and his friends. Rick's friends are sitting at the table smoking and drinking while watching football and the kids are in their bedroom playing. At Grandma's house Louis left and Marvin stayed. He wanted to talk to Grandma alone. Sitting outside on the porch, "Grandma It's hard. I can't find a job nowhere. I'm doing everything right. I'm putting God first, I'm praying, and things are not working out. Marvin, shaking his head, "When I see Louis and them making money and I can't even buy a soda, it makes me think that people that's doing wrong are the ones getting ahead."

"Marvin, you just keep praying and always put God first in everything you do. How is your faith? You have to believe and know that God is going to make a way. Be patient honey. Sometimes we want our plans to go our way when we want it to. But Gods way could mean different plans for us at a different time. Believe me, if you keep doing the right thing, you will be blessed with a job that God wants you to have." "Ok thanks Grandma, I knew you would have an answer." Marvin smiling, "O yeah, Grandma would you mind if I stayed here? I don't need to be around Louis and them." "Of course, Lisa and the kids are gone so you can have her room.

It's 5:00 pm and Robin is just waking up after singing all weekend at the club. She jumps up because she has to be at the band meeting at 5:30 to get paid. She arrives to the meeting at 5:45 and hears loud talking. The band is celebrating their new singer. She walks in and everyone is telling her what a good job she did this weekend. Robin is very happy to hear that everything went well, but she was tired from being out all weekend, she tells another singer name Sandy, "I have to get use to this, my body feels drained." Sandy giggles, "It's your first weekend girl, you'll get used to it. We all went through that." Sandy reaches in her purse, "you want some of this." She pulls out a bag of cocaine. "I call it the energizer it wakes me up and keeps me going all day and night." Robin looks at Sandy like she is crazy, "Nah. Is that drugs? No thanks! I never done that before and never will." "Ok…., it helps me. Let me know if you change your mind."

It's Monday morning and everyone is starting their week. Kevin comes home after work and finds a note saying hi and love you from the two youngest kids but nothing from Jr. He is still angry and is hanging out with the wrong crowd at school.

Marvin is at the unemployment office job hunting at a time companies are laying off. Now his probation officer is telling him he has to find a job soon as possible to start paying his fines or he could go back to jail.

Troy is over Louis' house looking around trying to find out where Louis keeps his money. Troy doesn't find anything, but finds out that Louis get his car and truck detailed on Mondays around noon. Troy is thinking that Monday is a good time to break into Louis house and calls Scooter and Fat Frank to tell them his idea.

Lisa is getting ready for work, and Rick just woke up to talk to her before she leaves. Rick walks in the bathroom where she is, "Lisa I have to drop you off today I need to use the car." "Do what? Why?" "My cousin said his job is hiring and I want to put an application in." "Are you going to be by my job at five? I had to wait outside for an hour last time you had the car?" "I told you I was sorry, and it wouldn't happen again dang." "Well come on hurry up, I have to leave now."

Lisa gets to work five minutes late because Rick had to get dressed. Her co-worker sees her getting dropped off. One of her co-workers name Tanisha says out loud, "oh boy he's using her car again ya'll. I heard that he was using her car to ride some other girl around." Lisa walks in the office, "Hello everybody." Nobody said nothing. Lisa looks around "Is everything ok?" Everybody said yes, except Tanisha. "No, girl everything is not ok. I'm going to tell you your man is using you. I heard he was hanging over on the eastside with some girl in your car." "What? Tanisha you don't know what you talking about." "Ok, I'm out of it, but don't say I didn't warn you."

Meanwhile later in the day, it's almost six o'clock and Pastor Tim is on his way to Mr. Smith's house. He has now convinced himself that there is nothing wrong with having a cup of coffee and talking, and he feels that he is strong enough to avoid Tina. He pulls up to Mr. Smith's house and sees Tina car. Talking to himself, "I can handle this." While walking up to Mr. Smith's door, Tina is standing at the door with a smile, "Well hello there Tim. I see you like my coffee." Tina opens the door, "come on in, my father is sleeping." Pastor Tim looking confused about going inside, "only for a second Tina."

Pastor Tim goes into the living room and sits down in the same spot he did before, waiting for his coffee. Sitting there, he starts to wonder how the evening is going to go and what will him and Tina talk about now that she knows he is attracted to her. Minutes later, Tina walks in the living room without his coffee and grabs Pastor Tim by the hand and he gets up and she walks him down the hall into the guess room and closed the door.

Meanwhile at Kevin's and Kim's house Marvin and Jr. are at the dining room table talking. Kim had asked Marvin to talk to Jr. because he got in trouble at school. Marvin sat at the table with his fingers crossed and Jr. has a look on his face like, what you want. "Ok Jr. what's going on man? Talk to me." "I'm not going to let nobody punk me." "Man you got it all wrong. You have to walk away if you can. Life is going to bring you situations and you have to handle them the right way so you won't be getting yourself in any trouble." Jr. looks at Marvin, "you used to be tough, you didn't let nobody punk you." "Yeah, used to be and look where it got me man, in jail. Now I know life rules. God gives us rules to live by and if you follow those rules you'll know how to handle trouble when it comes." Jr. gets angry, "man you don't even have a job, so how you going to talk to me about life. You and Louis sold drugs, messed up people's lives, and you want to talk to me about life." Jr. left the house to go hang with his friends while Marvin stayed behind and prays for him with Michelle.

Meanwhile at Lisa's job, Rick picks up Lisa from work fifteen minutes late. On the way to get the kids from daycare, Lisa is curious about what Tanisha said about Rick, so she just blurts out, "Rick, this girl on my job named Tanisha said that you been hanging with some girl in DC with my car. Is that true?" "What? Who is Tanisha? She don't know me. She must got the car mix up with somebody else." Rick has a smirk on his face shaking his head, "that's wrong, I can't believe you asked me that. All I do is job hunt all day. It sounds like to me somebody don't want to see you happy baby." "Well maybe she got the car mix up or something. Sorry I shouldn't have said anything, but it was on my mind all day. I had to at least ask you." "It's alright, but tell your co-worker to stop spreading rumors."

Days later and everyone is going on with life…

It's Friday, and Pastor Tim and Tina have been going out every night and keeping in touch. He calls her and she calls him. He is comfortable with seeing her, and now he feels no guilt or shame about being with Tina. He acts as if she was his wife.

At Troy's apartment, Troy is talking to Scooter and Fat Frank, "Louis is gone almost all day on Mondays detailing his truck and stuff, and that's a good day to break in his house." So they agreed that Monday was good.

At Kevin's house, Jr. is skipping school now to hanging out with his friends. Kevin and Kim have no idea.

The day is gone and Robin had just finished getting herself together to perform tonight. Not used to working in the day and singing at night in the clubs, she was exhausted. When she arrives at the club, she notices that the place is already packed. So she starts feeling that she has to wake up and really perform. Worried about being tired and performing in front of a packed place, she walks around the club looking for Sandy. Robin sees Sandy sitting at the end of the bar talking to a man. She walks up behind Sandy and taps her on the shoulder. Sandy with a drink in her hand turns around, "hey girl, how are you? You ready?" "Girl I'm tired." "Yeah... you better wake up. We're going to have to jam tonight and I hear that some key people are here." The man sitting at the bar with Sandy looks at her, "are you going to introduce me to you friend?" "Oh yeah, Robin this is my friend Bobby, and Bobby this is our new singer Robin." Bobby puts out his hand to Robin for a hand shake, "hello my name is Bobby but my friends call me BB." Sandy looks at her watch, "ok Robin it almost that time. We better go in the back." Robin watches Sandy give Bobby some money and Bobby hands her a small bag. Sandy stands up and grabs Robin by the hand and they walk into the bathroom before meeting the group in the back. In the bathroom looking in the mirror Robin is curious, as she looks at Sandy, "does that stuff really help you perform?" "What stuff?" "You know, the stuff in that bag that BB gave you." Sandy reaching in her purse to get the bag, "you talking about this? Here, try it and see for yourself, you'll be ok." "It won't have me looking crazy, will it?" "No girl, here try it. I bet you will perform better than ever." "Well let me see it." It's the end of the show and everything went well. Robin was energized and turned it out.

Waking up the next morning after only sleeping for a few hours, Robin feels excited about her performance last night. She calls Sandy and leaves a message on her phone. "Wake up girl, I just wanted to say thanks for the energizer," Then she laughs, "last night, it really helped me, and I felt great. Talk to you later." Robin didn't feel bad like she thought she would. After hearing all her life to stay away from drugs, she didn't see anything wrong with it after trying it last night. Now she thinks that she can handle cocaine and she wants her own personal bag to help her perform.

At Grandma's house, the unemployment office sent Marvin a job fair letter in the mail. Marvin is excited, thinking this could be his breakthrough. He starts making arrangements to go to the job fair on Monday so he calls Louis to see if Louis is interested. "Hey Louis what's up man, what you doing?" "Nuttin man just chilling." "Hey checks this out, what you doing Monday?" "On Monday,

I get the rides detailed?" "Check this out, there is a job fair down town Monday, and we need to go." Louis not interested, "man you know that job thing isn't for me, that's for you! Tell you what if you need a ride you can borrow the car. The truck is in the shop and I'll get it detailed later, oh yeah you had a phone call yesterday from some guy name Leon. He said that you would know who he is, I wrote his number down."

Marvin gets quiet, he remembers Leon from prison, but he doesn't tell Louis who he is, "Ok I'll get that number from you later." It's Sunday morning, and everybody is in church except Kevin and Lisa. Kevin had to work, and Lisa was up late with her boyfriend and his friends. The day went by and Marvin went with Louis to spend the night so he could use Louis' car.

It's Monday morning, and Marvin gets up early. First he thanks God and then he prays about getting a job at the job fair today. He wants to leave early because he knows a lot of people will be there. After getting dressed, he goes in the kitchen to get something to drink, and then he grabs the keys. Before leaving, he peeps in Louis room, only to see Louis still sleep. Marvin picks up his resumes' off the table and heads out the door.

Hours later at Troy's apartment, Troy is on the phone talking to Scooter, "ok yall up and ready." "Yeah we were waiting to hear from you." "Ok, meet me at my apartment around ten and we can roll out. Louis leaves his house around eleven." Troy's at his apartment sitting on the couch watching TV waiting for Scooter and Fat Frank to get there, but now he starts having second thoughts. Then he hears a knock at the door. Looking at the time, it's ten o'clock. Troy answers the door and lets the guys in. Troy doesn't feel right because of how close him and Louis been for years, "man I'm having second thoughts. I don't know, me and Louis go way back."

Fat Frank looks at Troy, "man if he was that tight with us he wouldn't have treated us like that." Then Troy starts to think about what happened. "Yeah you right, let's do it." While Scooter and Fat Frank are talking about what they're going to do with their share of the money, Fat Frank takes off his jacket and Troy sees a gun in Fat Franks belt. "Yo what's that for? I told you man no one is to get hurt, that's aight I'm not doing it." "Na bra, I always keep this on me". Troy gets mad, "you don't need it today? Man forget it I'm not going, we don't need no gun." "Ok, ok I'll leave the gun, man! I'll put it in the car." Troy shakes his head, "thank you. Ok y'all its almost 10:40, what y'all want to do?" "Let's go."

Meanwhile its 11:00 and Troy drove past Louis' house looking around for his car. Troy doesn't see the car, "Ok good his car is gone, now is the time so let's move quick." Parking in the driveway, they get out the car and walked around the back to make sure no one is looking. Louis is in the basement, sitting back in the recliner watching TV, waiting to hear from Marvin. While flipping channels, Louis hears noise coming from the patio door. Louis gets up and walks over to the sliding glass doors to see what the noise was. He moves the curtain back at the sliding glass door and he sees Troy, Scooter and Fat Frank. Louis is surprised, thinking that they were playing a joke on him. He opens the sliding glass door and points his figure at them and says "bam gotcha" and laughs, "what y'all doing? Trying to scare me homie?" Troy was shocked to see Louis was home, they were at a loss of words and just stood still. Then Troy thinking fast speaks up, "yeah man we thought we could sneak up on you, but you caught us." Louis waving his hand, "come on in and stop playing." Louis turns around to walk back to the recliner and there's a loud bang, "POW" a gunshot sounds off.

Meanwhile at the unemployment office, Marvin was upset because he didn't find a job at the job fair so he left around noon. Disappointed about not getting a job, he rode over Renee's parents house to see if he could see little Marvin. Knocking on the door and again there's no answer but he sees both cars parked in the driveway. After numerous attempts, Marvin leaves a note with a contact number this time.

Walking back to the car, he calls Louis to let him know that he is on his way to bring him back his car back. There's no answer from the house phone, so he calls his cell phone and still no answer. Feeling hungry, Marvin looks in his wallet to how much money he has. Looking at two dollars in his wallet and feeling desperate for money, he sees Leon's phone number beside the two dollars. A thought about calling Leon and making some fast money crosses his mind. He's thinking that he could just do it one time and make a lot of cash and stop. But he closes his wallet and decides to go take Louis his car.

Marvin gets to Louis' house and knocks on the door, but there is no answer. Then he calls and there is no answer. He hears the TV on, so he decides to walk around back. When Marvin gets around back, he sees the sliding glass door open. He shouts "Louis, Louis, where you at man?" Then he walks in and finds Louis on the floor face down lying in blood.

Four Months Later...

It's December, Friday morning Grandpop and Marvin are sitting on the porch laughing and talking about when Marvin, Louis and Lisa were kids. Then Grandpop get serious. "You know Marvin I never told you, but I'm proud of you. You really have come a long way and made a change for the better. Before I didn't say much, because you and Louis were living a life style like no one could tell y'all anything and y'all thought y'all new everything about fast money, cars and partying. Grandpop shakes his head, "Sometimes life experience is the best teacher, that's if you get a second chance because of God's grace and mercy. I know right now you're going through because you have no job, but keep praying and keep the faith. You know those jobs that turn you down, God allowed it to happen. God will close doors and open much bigger ones that you can't explain, so every door closed is preparing you for that big one to open. But you got to keep the faith and keep reading his word and you will hear from Him, and He will direct your path. So don't give up, remember there's no right way in going the wrong way." Marvin listening, "Yeah Pops it is rough out here, it's been almost six months with no income, I can't pay y'all rent, I can't even buy food to eat. I owe y'all a lot, and I will pay y'all back." "Just keep right on doing what God wants you to do, and you will be blessed." Marvin laughs, "You and grandma think alike, she says the same thing." "After 40 something years of marriage, you would think alike too."

While Marvin and Grandpop are out on the porch, a car pulls up and yells Marvin name. "Marvin, Marvin, come here for a second." Not recognizing who it is, Marvin walks down the steps to the car and stoops down at the passenger window, and he can hardly recognize this person. Marvin is shocked, "Wow, what's up Robin, haven't seen you in months. I guess since you left the church, right?" "Yeahhh it's been awhile, you staying out of trouble?" "Yeah, I'm taking it one day at a time." Robin getting straight to the point, "hey you know anybody that got anything?" Marvin curious, "Anything like what?" "You know some coke or rock." Marvin is shocked but now he knows why he didn't recognize her, "some coke or rock? Girl what you talking about, you not messing with that stuff are you? I thought you were doing good singing and stuff." "Na, I quit the group, they were complaining too much for me. They tried to tell me that drugs were messing with me, I was late only a few times." Robin said laughing. Marvin shakes his head, "Robin, not you man. How long you have been messing with that stuff?" "Why? I'm ok it's not like I can't control it or something degg, who you my father?" "Well if you can stop, then stop. I'm telling you, it will take you for a ride that you don't need, and if you are not an addict, you will be soon." Robin is looking at Marvin like something is wrong with him, "I only want a $20 bag, is that asking too much?" "I tell you what Robin, if you not doing anything Sunday, come to church with me." "What?" Come to church with me Sunday, and I won't take no for an answer! Please come, I'm going to beg you till you say yes, please, please, please." Laughing Robin tells Marvin, "Stop playing boy." "Ok, I'll go but I can't go with you. I will meet you there." "Sounds good, ok I'll see you there."

Robin drives off and Marvin hears Grandma calling him to help her put Louis in his wheel chair. Louis now lives with grandma, he can't get around without a wheelchair, and he goes to physical therapy twice a week. Marvin runs in the house to help grandma get Louis out of bed and puts him in his wheelchair. Marvin rolls Louis out onto the porch with him and Grandpop. Grandpop looks at Louis, "how are you feeling this morning?" "I feel alright, the physical therapist said I'll be back walking in no time, and I can't wait." Louis grunting from being stiff, "I'll feel even better when I get dem jokers back. Marvin shaking his head at Louis, "you just don't get it do you? Man you need to let it go and move on and thank God you still living. The doctor said that the bullet just missed your spine, this is what I was telling you this junk isn't worth your life cuz." "If I don't get' em back, I'll be looking like a punk in the streets. Then everybody will try me, and how will I make money like that, if people think I'm weak ha?" Marvin puts his hands over his face and looks at Louis, "dude just do me one favor."

"What?" "Come to church with me Sunday, and I won't take no for an answer. Today is Friday and you have two days to get yourself together so no excuses man." "Yeah I'll go, as long as someone helps me in this wheel chair, I was planning on going in the first place."

Meanwhile at Lisa's job, Lisa has been feeling sick and nausea for almost two weeks. Thinking she might be pregnant, she brought a test. Excited about being pregnant by her boyfriend Rick, she goes in the restroom smiling and takes her pregnancy test. The test is positive, Lisa is pregnant, and she's excited and happy and can't wait to tell Rick. Now they can get married and be the family she always wanted. Excited, she rushes out the restroom back to her desk smiling. The women in the office are wondering what is going on, but no one asks. Tanisha gets up and walks over to Lisa. "Ok girl I'm not scared to ask, did you hit the lottery or something? What's going on with you?" Lisa says nothing for 5 minutes, she just smiles at Tanisha. After Tanisha kept picking, Lisa finally says something, "no I didn't hit the lottery, I got something better." Lisa still smiling, "I am pregnant, and my baby and I are going to get married." "Ahhh, congratulations Lisa, girl you better invite me to the wedding." Then Lisa says it out loud so the entire office can hear her, "I'm pregnant and I'm getting married." Lisa gets her cell phone and goes to the break room to call Rick. "Hello." Lisa excited, "hi baby, are you busy?" "No, what up? Why you so happy?" "I have a surprise for you but I want to wait to tell you so I can see your face." "What?" What is it, you know I hate surprises. You all excited and stuff, you hit the lottery or something?" "Noooo, no lottery." Lisa laughs, "something better than that." "Come on now, you shouldn't have called me if you're not planning on telling me. You know I hate that stuff deg, bye." "Ok ok, I'll tell you, welllllllll you arreeeee, I mean me, well we are going to have a baby. Baby I'm pregnant." Rick gets quiet and doesn't say anything for minutes. There is silence from him while Lisa is talking. Lisa realizes that Rick isn't saying anything, "Baby did you hear me, we're having a baby." "Are you sure it's mine?" "What?" "What are you talking about, stop playing boy?" "Lisa I'm not playing, I can't have kids right now." "Huh, a little too late for that mister so stop worrying, we will be ok. You still getting that job with your cousin and I have a good job so stop we will be ok." Rick hesitates, "Lisa that's not what I'm talking about, what I'm trying to say is that, we're not going to be together." Lisa gets serious, "Stop playing with me Rick. What are you talking about?"

"I don't know how to say this, but remember your co-worker was telling you about me riding another girl in the car from the eastside? Well that was my baby's mother and we're thinking about getting back together. I was going to tell you, but anyway, I'm sorry Lisa. You can't be pregnant by me, I didn't mean for this to happen. I'm sure you will find another man. Lisa is trying to talk but she is having an anxiety attack "Wha, wha, what?" Lisa drops the phone crying in disbelief and screams, "no no no." Tanisha hears her and comes in the break room. "Honey you ok?" Not answering, Lisa is on the floor holding her stomach crying, and trying to catch her breath and keep saying, "no." Tanisha sees that something is wrong and picks up her phone and looks in the contacts and sees grandma's phone number. Tanisha pushed the call button. Marvin answers the phone. "Hello." "Hello my name is Tanisha and I work with Lisa, I believe she might need someone to come and get her. "Why? "Is she ok?" "Sir, I don't think so. She won't stop crying long enough to talk, someone needs to come get her." "Ok, thank you.

Tell her I'm on my way." Tanisha hangs up the phone and wraps her arms around Lisa, telling her, "It's going to ok."

Marvin gets to Lisa's job and Lisa is still crying and won't talk to nobody. She can't believe what just happened to her. She is confused and can't help but to wonder if this is a dream. She gets in the car with help from Tanisha and balls up in a knot still holding her stomach. Marvin looks at Lisa, "what's wrong?" "You want to talk about it?" Lisa still not talking and Marvin gets concerned, "do you want to go to your apartment?" Lisa nods her head yes, "I don't want to be around nobody right now. I want to be alone." Lisa's now having thoughts of suicide. "Ok you're talking now, can you tell me what's wrong, and if you want to talk about it? I'm a good listener." "No." Then seconds later she screams, "I am so stupid." "No you're not, don't say that. Whatever happened to you can be fixed." Lisa's still screaming, "Marvin, I'm pregnant and Rick said it can't be his because him and his baby's mother are getting back together." Lisa starts crying again. Marvin, concerned makes a u-turn, "I'm taking you over grandma's house. You don't need to be alone right now. I won't say anything to nobody about what you just told me, you can just go lay down."

They get to grandma's house and Lisa says nothing to nobody. She went straight to the bedroom to lie down. Louis and Grandpop are looking at Marvin waiting for him to say something about Lisa. He just shrugs his shoulders. Grandma asks Marvin, "What's wrong with Lisa?" "Grandma I rather let Lisa tell ya'll what's going on, it's not my place to put her business out there." It's almost 6:30pm on Friday evening. Lisa woke up and came out of the bedroom. Still upset, she asked Marvin, "Did you say anything?" "Nah, I told you I wasn't going to say nothing, but you need to say something to grandma. She's worried about you and the kids." "Oh my kids, I have to go get them." "I already got them, they're out front playing. Look at you, you forgot about your kids." "Don't let no man get you so angry that you forget your kids Lisa." "It's not like that, I just lost track of time." "Well you need to get yourself together for those kids. I tell you what, do me a favor." "What?" "Come with me to church Sunday." "I need to do something, ok I'll go."

Later on that night...

Its 10:10pm, Kevin is at work, and Kim is at home with the two youngest kids. She doesn't know where Jr. is. Kim is watching TV while the kids are lying on the couch falling asleep. Then the phone rings. Kim, thinking it might be Kevin, gets up and answers the phone. "Hello." "Hello, my name is officer Williams, I'm with the county police department and I have a young man here by name of Kevin Jones Jr. and he gave me this number to call." "Are you his mother?" "Yes I am." "Is everything ok?" "He and his friends were joy riding in a stolen car, and the other two boys got away." "He did what?" "I can't believe this, what is wrong with this boy." "Mrs. Jones he is being released on his own conduct. We know that he didn't steal the car, he was in the back seat and he couldn't get out and run. But he will have to appear in court two weeks from now. He has all the paper work with his court date." Kim nervous and scared, "is he in trouble? Can I speak to him?" "Sorry Mrs. Jones, right now he is in the youth block and if he is in trouble or not is up to the judge. I'm sure the investigator will want him to tell us who the other two boys are. What I need now is for an adult to come and sign for his release and pick him up before 11." Kim is really confused and scared for Jr. She starts to leave, but she knows she is in no shape to drive. Pacing the floor, she calls Kevin and he doesn't answer his phone.

At the jail, Jr. is in the youth block scared. The youth block is a huge room full of bunk beds in the center of the room. There are 33 teen boys in this block and Jr. knows no one. One of the boys keeps looking at Jr. He recognizes Jr. from being with a gang of boys that tried to jump him at a high school game one night. The boy finally approaches Jr, "hey I remember you, you and your boys tried to jump me at a football game." Jr. remembers the boy, now he is really scared for his life. "Hey that wasn't me that was the boy I was with." "I don't care, you was with him so you got to pay." Jr., walking backwards, sits on the floor with his back against the wall. He watches the boy walking around the room whispering to other teens, and pointing at him.

Kim is at home still trying to call Kevin and still no answer, so she calls grandma's house. Louis and Marvin are up watching TV when the phone rings. "Hello." Kim is hysterical and not making sense, "Marvin, Marvin you have to help me. I'm at home with the kids and Kevin is at work and Jr. is in jail." "What, what happened?" "I'll explain later, I need someone to go pick him up before eleven." "It's quarter till, I'll try to be there by eleven, plus I can't sign him out cause of my felony charge. I'll bring grandma with me." Back at the jail in the youth block, four boys keep looking at Jr. and one of them lifted up his shirt and shows Jr. a homemade knife. Jr. looks at the clock and its eleven o'clock and bed time is in a half hour. Jr. knows he can't go to sleep around these boys.

A half hour went by and Jr. is scared and nervous and keeps looking at the clock. Its eleven thirty, and the guard came in the dorm to do his walk around and head count while telling everyone its bed time. Then the TV cuts off and the guard tells the boys again, "get in bed." As the guard leaves the room he turns off the lights from outside the room, and locks the door. Jr. is lying in bed scared with tears running down his face. He looks around to see if anybody is coming and he sees the boy with the knife looking at him. Laying on his back, he puts his pillow over his chest and then the lights come back on and the guard opens the door and shouts, "Kevin Jones Jr. gather your things and come up front." Jr. jumps up out of bed and runs up front leaving his belongings behind. He just wants to get out of there.

Marvin and grandma took Jr. home. When they pulled up, Kim is at the front door waiting for them. Marvin walks Jr. to the house, and Kim met them at the door with her arms folded while screaming at Jr. "You better tell who the other two boys are, or you are going to get it. Marvin looks at Jr. and shakes his head, "yeah, you're put between a rock and a hard place. If you tell on those boys, they will get you and if you don't they will put it all on you. Man this is what I was trying to tell you, anyway we will think of something. I have to go take grandma home, call me in the morning!"

Marvin and grandma are heading home. Marvin calls Kevin's cell phone. Kevin finally picks up, "hello." "Hey man where you been? Your wife has been trying to call you." "Why? What's wrong?" "Jr. had gotten locked up, hanging with some boys in a stolen car." "Jr. who, not my boy Jr. He don't hang with a crowd like that." "Man you been working so much you don't know what's going on at your house. Your son needs you right now, not later, not tomorrow but right now. At least call your wife." "Ok, ok, I got to go, let me call Kim." Kevin calls Kim. Kim is upset while explaining to Kevin about what happened to Jr. Kevin can't believe what he is hearing about Jr. Kim's arguing with Kevin, "you are not around. You don't know what's going on around here." "How come you never told me this stuff before?" "Look, I tried Kevin, and don't try to put this on me." Kevin hangs up his cell phone and tells the other supervisor he has an emergency and has to go home. Running to his car, Kevin leaves work in a hurry. When Kevin gets home he is furious and storms in the house and goes upstairs to jump on Jr. Kim puts her arm across Jr.'s door and stops him. "Kevin don't you dare jump on that boy, you are part of this problem." "What you talking about? How am I part of the problem?" "You're never here and Jr. has been hanging out with these boys for months now and his grades have dropped and everything. He needs his father not a gang of boys. Please talk to him. He is already mad at you. He thinks that you care more about work than him." "Why didn't you tell me about all this before?" "I tried, but you are so hooked up in your job. We don't exist. I'm here raising these kids by myself and Jr. is at the age that he needs a father.

Marvin and grandma help out when you're not around, but it's not you."

After talking to Kim and feeling bad, Kevin goes in Jr.'s room to talk to him, but Jr. had cried himself to sleep. So Kevin went back downstairs and goes into the kitchen to call Marvin and thank him for everything he has done. Marvin half sleep, "Hello." Kevin sniffing from crying, and upset about what Kim had told him, Hey Marvin, I don't mean to call so late. But I just want to thank you man for being there for my family man." "No problem man, we all are in this together." "Well you go on back to sleep and I'll get with you later." "Hey, hey umm Kevin, do me a favor." "What?" "I know you work Sunday night and you need your rest, but if you can come to church Sunday that would be nice." "Sure, sure I'll be there, go back to sleep man."

4 hours later…

It is 5:30 a.m. Saturday morning, Grandpop is up out of bed. He gets up early every morning. While Grandpop is in the kitchen making his famous coffee he hears a hard knock at the door, then the doorbell rings, then another knock.

Grandpop is wondering who could be knocking at the door this time of morning like that. He goes to the window and peeps out of the side of the curtain, he sees a detective car and a plain dressed man at the door, Grandpop opens the door slightly with the chain locked. "May I help you sir." "Morning sir, sorry to bother you this time of morning, but I'm looking for a gentlemen by the name of Marvin Anderson I'm his probation officer." "Ok, one moment please." Grandpop closes the door. Walking down the hall to Marvin's bedroom, Grandpop knocked on the door. Marvin wakes up moving slow, he answers, "what now?" "Marvin your probation officer is at the front door, and he wants to see you." Marvin gets up out of bed, and put his clothes on, and rushes down the hall to open the door. Opening the door, "hey Mr. Hawcoms, what brings you by this time of morning?" "Nothing, just making my rounds, how are you coming along?" "I'm doing good, just haven't found a job yet." "Are you looking, it's been almost six months now, you can work at a fast food or anywhere. I know it's not the money that you want, but you need to start paying on your fines, or I have to bring you back to court. And why your eyes look like that? You been hanging out all night?" "No, no I umm, haven't had much sleep, there was a family issue and I had just went to bed a couple of hours ago." Mr. Hawcoms thinks that Marvin is lying. He thinks that Marvin has been hanging out with his old crowd again. "Do I need to give you a drug test Marvin?" "That's up to you Mr. Hawcoms, I'm clean. I have no problem with taken a test." "Well, I don't have any on me now, but I will give you one later. Let me tell you something Marvin, I don't know what you're doing, but you better stop doing it or I will have to give you those six years back, you hear me." "What you talking about Mr. Hawcoms?" Mr. Hawcoms whispering to Marvin, "I have been doing this for years, and I seen you guys come and go. I know how you young punks think. Y'all think y'all are slick, and can get away with not working and hanging out dealing your drugs. Then you wind up back in jail and it will be just a matter of time before you hang yourself. I tell you what, I am going to leave now so you can go back to sleep, but I'm going to give you a time limit to get a job. Call me on Monday and I will give you your deadline date and I might put you on a curfew, then you won't be hanging out all night." Marvin is listening and wondering what is Mr. Hawcoms is talking about. Mr. Hawcoms leaves and Marvin is in the living room sitting in the chair staring at the wall trying to figure out what just happened. Grandpop walks in the living room and sees Marvin staring at the wall. "You ok son?" "No Pops I'm not, I'm doing my best to do the right thing. I'm job hunting every day. I'm doing all this just to have my probation officer tell me I'm lying and I could go back to jail for 6 years. I might as well go back to the streets if I am getting blamed for it." "You mean that you're going to give up just like that. You let that man come in here for 20 minutes and change what God has planned for you. You stay focused and as long as you are on God's team, no man can do anything to you. God is testing your faith son. You can't give up every time things don't look right. Where's your faith? Go get your Bible." Marvin goes to his room and gets his Bible. Grandpop tells Marvin, let's read 1 Peter 1:7. It says: these trials will show that your faith is genuine. It is being tested as fire tests and purifies gold—though your faith is far more precious than mere gold. So when your faith remains strong through many trials, it will bring you much praise and glory and honor on the day when Jesus Christ is revealed to the whole world. "You're right Pop, thanks, my God will work it out. And I will turn it all over to Him. Now I can lie down without worrying, thanks."

Its nine o'clock, and Grandma is cooking breakfast, the smell from the kitchen gets everybody out of bed. That's her way of waking them up on Saturday mornings. Lisa and the kids come in the kitchen first while wiping their eyes, "good morning Grandma." Grandma looks at Lisa, "good morning, I see you feeling better." Grandma didn't give Lisa a chance to say anything, "honey is everything ok." Lisa peeps out of the kitchen to see if anybody was coming. Then she took a deep breath, trying not to cry, "Grandma I'm pregnant and my boyfriend Rick said it's not his. I don't know what to do."

Grandma sits down beside her and holds her hand, "first of all that's your ex boyfriend. You don't need a boy like that, and it's going to be alright. But, Lisa you are going to have to stop falling so easy for these boys. Just because a man says he loves you, doesn't mean he loves you." "I know Grandma, but I always give them my all, just to get hurt." Lisa hears Louis and Marvin coming, "I'll talk to you later, Louis and Marvin are coming." Marvin pushes Louis in his wheelchair into the kitchen. "Good morning Grandma." "Good morning boys. I need y'all to clean the kitchen when y'all finish eating. I have to go pick up Grandpop's medicine."

Meanwhile at Kevin and Kim's house, Kevin calls Jr. to come downstairs to talk to him. Kevin wants to know what's been going on with Jr. He comes walking down stairs and sat on the couch. Kevin is pacing the floor, then sits down beside Jr. Right before he starts to talk the doorbell rang. Kevin gets back up and answers the door, "Hello, may I help you?" "Good morning sir, my name is Detective Pearson. I'm investigating a Kevin Jones Jr. case." Kevin shakes Detective Pearson's hand, "come on in Detective, my son and I was just getting ready to have a talk. What can we help you with?" "Well I just have a few questions to ask your son about his case." "No problem." Kevin walks Detective Pearson into the living room and introduces him to Jr. and explains why he's there. Then they all went to the dining room table and sat down. Detective Pearson pulls out his notepad and ink pen and started asking questions. "Ok Jr., the car that you and your friends were riding in was stolen, did you know that?" "No." "How many persons were in the car including yourself?" "Three." "Whose car did you think it was?" Kevin interrupts Detective

Pearson. "Hold it detective, are you trying to trick Jr. into giving you the names of the other two boys?" "Look Mr. Jones, I will put it to you like this, if he doesn't give up the other two boys, Jr. will be charged with the stolen car. Not only that, the owner of the car was assaulted, he was hit in the back of the head with an unidentified object. So it's up to you all if Jr. gets locked up or not." "Ok Detective, I think it's time we get a lawyer, and you can talk to him." "You do what you have to do, but if you work with us you don't need a lawyer. You can save yourself some time and money." Kevin is concerned, "before Jr. gives any names, I need to find out what kind of people we are dealing with. These guys could be the type of people that comes after my family if Jr. gives you their names and I don't need that Detective." "Like I said, you do what you have to do. Here is my card. If you want to talk, give me a call." Detective Pearson looks at Jr., "oh, one more question. You don't have to answer me if you don't want to, but does the name Butch sound familiar?" Jr. gets this real strange blank look on his face and looks at Kevin, but doesn't say anything. Kevin can tell that something is wrong when the name Butch was mentioned. Kevin walks Detective Pearson to the door. He stands out front of his house watching Detective Pearson as he drives off. Shaking his head, he walks back in the house and sits by Jr. Kevin is curious. "Jr., who is Butch?" "Butch is the boy that was driving the car."

Meanwhile at Robin's apartment, Robin had just got in from yesterday. She was out all night smoking crack cocaine and spent all her money from her pay check. Wanting something to drink, she goes in the kitchen and opens the refrigerator door and it's off. Thinking that it's broken, she closes the door and walks back into the living room. Then she grabs the remote control off the table and pushes the ON button, and the TV doesn't come on, then she realizes that her electric was off. Looking for her electric bill, she goes through a stack of mail on the table. She thought about calling the power company to make payment arrangements, but her phone was turned off last week. Realizing that there is nothing she can do and feeling tired, she lies on the couch and falls asleep.

Later that day around five o'clock that evening, Pastor Tim and Tina are at a restaurant having dinner together and afterwards they plan on checking out a movie. During dinner, Pastor

Tim's cell phone rings. He looks at the caller ID and sees that it's Marvin. "Hey Marvin, what's up." "Hey Pastor Tim, are you busy?" "A little, I'm having dinner right now. Is everything ok?" "Yeah everything is good. I wanted to call you and let you know that I had invited Robin, Louis, and Kevin to church tomorrow. I was wondering if you could talk to them about dealing with life and the consequences that come from the choices that we make." Rushing Marvin off the phone, "sure, sure Marvin, I would love too. Thanks for the call, I'm going to get back to my dinner before it gets cold ok."

Marvin hangs up the phone and starts to think about little Marvin. Wanting to see his son, Marvin gets Louis' car and drives over to Renee's parent's house again. This time while pulling up in front of the house the door is open. Excited Marvin gets out the car and runs to the front door. He rings the doorbell. He smells food cooking and rings the doorbell again. Marvin sees a little boy come running out of the kitchen by himself. Then, twenty seconds later Renee's mother came out of the kitchen behind the boy. She answers the door. "Well hello there Mr. Anderson, how are you doing?" "I'm doing good Mrs. Bell, it been a long time." Marvin looking at the little boy, "Mrs. Bell is that my son?" "Yes Marvin, that's little Marvin." Standing still staring at little Marvin, Marvin picks him up and hugs him. With tears coming down his face, Marvin sits down on the couch with little Marvin on his lap. "Mrs. Bell I been coming by here for almost six months looking for little Marvin." "I know Marvin we were here but my husband doesn't want you around little Marvin. I've talked to him over and over again asking him to let you be part of little Marvin's life. But my husband is scared. He doesn't want his grandson growing up around the drugs and violence. He lost a daughter and he doesn't want to lose his grandson." "Mrs. Bell I don't blame Mr. Bell, but I'm a changed person now. That life is behind me. God directs my path now." "Well that's good Marvin. Just let your talk back up your walk because everybody says the same thing when they are just getting out of jail. If you are really a changed man, I'm sure my husband will come around. Marvin I don't want to rush your visit but Mr. Bell should be home any minute now and I don't want any problems." "Ok Mrs. Bell, I understand. I don't want any problems either. Thanks for everything. Please continue to talk to Mr. Bell for me and I will do my part."

Marvin stands up and kisses lil Marvin and stares at a picture of Renee before leaving.

Excited about seeing his son, Marvin is praying while driving that Mr. Bell would come around, then his cell phone rings. "Hello." "Marvin, where are you?" "Who is this?" "Louis man, you don't know my voice? Grandma wants you to go by the store on your way back to get a loaf of bread." "Ok I got it. Hey, I just saw little Marvin man and he looks just like me." Meanwhile, it's the edge of dark, and Marvin gets to the store. Walking inside the grocery store, Marvin passes the cash registers heading towards the bread isle. He doesn't see Bobby in line watching him. Standing in line with his girlfriend, he starts to hide behind her. He grabs her arm and puts down the basket and pulls her out the store. "Bobby what going on, what are you doing? "Get in the car and start it." "What? What's going on?" Bobby's looking through the store window at Marvin standing in line at the cash register. He pulls out his gun and waits for Marvin to come out the store. Bobby hides behind the car parked beside Marvin. Still excited, Marvin walks out the store whistling. Headed toward the car he pushes the door open button on the keychain. Marvin reaches for the door handle and Bobby walks up behind him and puts the gun to Marvin's back. He dropped the keys and bread and put his hands up. "Hey man you can have the car, please don't shoot." "I don't want your car. I heard that you were looking for me." Marvin recognizes the voice, "Bobby is that you?" Bobby pushed the gun in Marvin's back and pulled the trigger (click, click), the gun jammed. Bobby dropped the gun and ran to his car, Marvin runs behind him. Bobby jumps in the car while screaming, "go, go, go, go," His girlfriend doesn't know what is going on. Scared and nervous, she can't drive, so she doesn't move the car. Marvin walks to the passenger side and knocked on the window, then he put his hands up. "Bobby, Bobby let me talk to you man. Calm down and let's talk." Scared thinking Marvin wants revenge, he screams through the window while it's up. "Marvin I'm sorry man. I didn't mean to set you up man." Marvin putting his hands up in the air, "Bobby I just want to talk to you man. Wind the window down." Bobby winds down the window halfway as Marvin tries to talk. "Dude I forgave you a long time ago. Going to jail helped me, it was part of Gods plan. Calm down and let's talk." Bobby's girlfriend gets herself together then she slams on the gas and pulls off while Marvin is standing there talking. Marvin watches them leave the parking lot then picks up the gun that Bobby dropped and runs inside the store to give to the security guard.

Meanwhile at Robin's apartment, Robin has to find somewhere to spend the night. She has no heat and its 38 degrees outside. She packs a small bag of clothes to go over her mother's house. When she gets in the car, the gas light is on, and she has no money. Desperate she starts knocking on her neighbor's doors begging for gas money. Finally after knocking on all the doors but one Robin gives up. Then an elderly lady opens the one door that she didn't knock on. "Here miss, here is a twenty dollar bill. Get you some gasoline, you hear?" Robin smiles. Feeling relieved, she grabs the twenty dollar bill, "thank you lady, I will pay you back, thank you."

Robin gets in her car and starts it up. Headed towards the gas station she looks at the twenty dollar bill and starts to thinks about a twenty dollar piece of crack. Battling in her mind, Robin turns her car around and goes gets crack. Returning back to her apartment with a flashlight, she gets her pipe to smoke. Sitting in the dark at the dining room table, her crack was gone and her high is gone. Wanting more she is on the floor with the flashlight tasting anything that looks like crack. After forty minutes on the floor in the dark with a flashlight, she realizes she has a problem and gets up and walks over to her couch and sits down. Balled up on the couch, she starts thinking. She has no electric, phone, heat, no gas in her car, and she spent the twenty dollars that the elderly lady gave her on crack. Feeling very depressed, it hits her that she has a big problem! Now having thoughts of suicide, she feels that she has nothing to lose.

Meanwhile at Grandma's house, Marvin gets there with the bread. Marvin tells Louis about what happened at the store with Bobby and how God saved his life because the gun jammed. Ready to go to her apartment, Lisa and the kids needs a ride home, her ex boyfriend texted her telling her that her car and keys are at her apartment. "Marvin can you take me and the kids home?" "Lisa, I just got in and I'm tired. Can you wait until tomorrow?" Lisa using church for an excuse, "well we can't go to church tomorrow if we can't go home. We need a change of clothes." "Ok, ok come on. But let's go now so I can get back here and do what I have to do."

147

Meanwhile at Kevin and Kim's house, Kevin asks Jr., "Can you find this boy Butch?" "Yeah, but Butch is not a boy, he's twenty years old." "Call him and let him know that you didn't say anything to the police, I have a family to protect." Jr. makes the call to Butch on his cell phone, Kevin is listening from another phone. Butch answers. "Hello." "Hey Butch, what's up man?" "Is this you youngin?" "Yeah." "You home? How you get out, you didn't snitch did you? "Na, na I would never do that? "So you didn't tell the police nothing?" "Na, I didn't say nothing." "I hope you telling me the truth youngin. I hate to see anybody get hurt, you know what I mean right?" "Na you don't have to worry about anything. I promise you man I didn't say nothing." After talking to Butch and trying to convince him that he didn't tell on him, Jr. hung up the phone. Kevin is hoping that Butch believes Jr. and goes in the living room with Kim and the kids and sits down.

The Next Day…

It's Sunday morning, and everybody is at church but Robin. Marvin sees Pastor Tim and walks over to him. Marvin whispered, "remember what I asked you on the phone yesterday?" Pastor Tim seems confused, "what?" "I invited Louis, Kevin, Lisa, and Robin to church today and they need to hear a word from God for direction, and I asked you if you could talk to them. Remember?" "Oh yeah, I remember, yes, yes, ok. I will talk to them after service, but I'm in a hurry. I have a date later."

Marvin, still looking around for Robin, sits down beside Grandma. He prayed that the church will get a message from God today about direction and which way God wants us to go. The choir started singing and people are up singing along and clapping their hands and Pastor Tim was is in the pulpit singing along with the choir song after song. The singing stopped and Pastor Tim stands up at the podium and tells the congregation, "good morning. It's ok to shout, dance, sing, and give praises, it's ok." Still talking to the congregation Pastor Tim asked, "Does anyone have a testimony to share or something to say? If so, please stand. Let's talk about the goodness of God."

Every Sunday, the same people stand up and give a testimony, but surprisingly today Pastor Tim's ex-wife Erica and his son stood up and waved but didn't say a word. They were just there to see how

Pastor Tim is coming along with ministry as Erica is considering giving him another chance. But another visitor stood up and had something to say. Everyone is looking at this visitor to see what he has to say, and he starts talking, "Well Pastor it's not really a testimony, it's a question." "Sure brother speak." "How long have you been seeing my wife Tina?" The church got silent, and then everyone started whispering. Then the congregation went into an uproar. People were shouting and yelling. Pastor Tim, embarrassed and ashamed, swiftly walks at a fast pace to his office and locked the door. One of the teenagers that Marvin talks to about life was sitting behind him and tapped him on the shoulder. "See Marvin, that's why I don't be listening to yall. There is a bunch of hypocrites in church." Marvin gets up and runs to Pastor Tim's office. Marvin knocks and knocks on the door, but he doesn't answer, so Marvin talks through the door. "Pastor Tim, are you ok?" He gets no answer. Grandma walks down the hall and sees Marvin at Pastor Tim's office knocking on the door, she tells Marvin, "You need to go out there and calm everybody down." "Me, how?" "You have a message from God that everyone needs to hear, pray about it."

Grandma leaves Marvin in the hallway, and she goes back to her seat. Marvin gets on his knees and prays for courage and a message from God to give to the congregation. The congregation is still in an uproar and is asking Tina's husband John questions, "What are you talking about?" John ignored the questions and walked out the church. During all the confusion, Robin walks in the church, looking around and wondering what's going on. She sits down in the back of the church. She looks rough, her hair is not done, her clothes are wrinkled and no one recognizes her. Robin is tired of the way her life is going and she came to church this morning hoping to get some help. Instead she hears about what happened and is more confused and thinking about leaving. Feeling that the church can't help her, Robin starts to get up to leave and she sees Marvin walk up to the pulpit. Approaching the podium, Marvin tells himself, "God did not give me the spirit of fear." At the podium, Marvin adjusts the microphone and tells the congregation "please listen, God has a message for the Church today." The Church still not listening he says it again, "please listen, God has a message for the Church today." People were getting up starting to leave, the choir members step down and sat in the congregation. Marvin sees people walking towards the exit door, and out of nowhere Marvin tells them, "Those of you who are leaving, this message is for you." One of the Church members shouted "you not a Pastor, you're an ex-con, and there is nothing that you can tell me." Humbling himself Marvin says, "Sorry that you feel that way, and no I'm not Pastor, but I have a message from God for you and the Church." Everyone but the man that shouted out had sat down to hear what Marvin had to say. Louis, Lisa, Kevin and his family had moved up front and Pastor Tim was listening from the speaker in his office. Marvin starts the message. "REPENT." "The Bible says in Act 3:19." Now repent of your sins and turn to God, so you're sins may be wiped away. "We are not including God in our everyday lives. We are making our own decisions. We are thinking for ourselves. We are taking our own directions. We are doing everything our way." Everyone was paying attention to the message. They know what they are hearing is from God, and not Marvin. After thirty minutes, Marvin ends the message. "Church, we lost focus on who God is, and once we did that our lives became total chaos. We made ourselves, people, money, job, objects, sex, and anything that we put before God, our God." "God gave us instructions on how to live." "God knows we are going to make mistakes, but he wants us to repent. It's when we don't repent from our sins, that we are headed for destruction." "If you know that you are not living right, and you want to make it right come to God. If you are tired of living in chaos, come up front, come to God. If you are ready to put your life in order, then come. Come to God, we must pray together. Don't let shame and guilt keep you in bondage, God already forgave you. You have been forgiven." "No matter what it is, God accepts you how you are. Mark 2:17 says, "It is not the healthy who need a doctor, but the sick. I have not come to call the righteous, but sinners." "God is inviting all of us. All we have to do is come to him. Come up front, and let's pray."

People started getting up and walking to the front. Pastor Tim came out his office and walked up front. Jr. walked up front, Louis with tears in his eyes went up front. Kevin and his family walked up front, and Lisa stayed in her seat crying. Half of the congregation came up for prayer to repent and get strength to stay focused. In the middle of the prayer they heard a beautiful voice coming from the back of the church, singing "Help me Lord, help me Lord." She kept singing this over and over again. She stood up still singing, with tears coming down her face. As she starts walking up front, people started whispering, "that looks like Robin." Robin is walking up front crying and singing "Help me Lord." Marvin recognizes Robin and meets her half way and hugs her and everybody in the church are on their feet rejoicing and praising. Then everyone came up front, held hands and prayed together.

The next day...

Monday morning, Marvin gets up and gets dressed to go job hunting, but he can't leave the house until his probation officer calls him. While Marvin is waiting for his phone call, Louis came in the living room to talk to him. "Marvin, I've never seen you like I did yesterday. You are taking this church thing serious." "I'm taking my relationship with God serious." "You know since you been home, I've seen a change in you. You seem to be at peace, have joy, and you are happy all the time. I want to have that peace, and happiness!" "Louis, it's because of my relationship with God that I have peace, joy, and happiness. I used to make money my god, and money got you shot in the back and got me locked up. Those are just some of the things that happened when we made money our god. That doesn't sound like peace and joy to me." Marvin shouted with joy! "Don't get me wrong, there is nothing wrong with having money, but you don't have to make it your god." Louis looked at how happy Marvin is, "I want that!" "What?" "Peace, joy, and happiness, man look at me. I was shot in the back, now I'm in a wheel chair. I'm not happy and I think about getting Troy and them back all the time. I have no peace man." "First of all, I give glory to God that you see something in me that makes you want to get some! Thank you Lord, but I'm going to tell you something. You are going to have to stay in the word because I battle everyday all day. It might look easy, but it's not easy. It's really hard when temptation surrounds you every day. There are many times that my flesh rises and I want to do what I want to do. That's why I have to stay reminded of who God is. Believe me cuz, God delivered me from one bondage, and the enemy put me in another that God is working on now. I'm not perfect by a long shot, but I am better off than what I use to be."

While Louis and Marvin are talking, the phone rings. Marvin looked at the clock it was 9 0'clock. Marvin answers the phone, "Hello." "Hello may I speak to a Marvin Anderson." "It's me Mr. Hawcoms." "Well Marvin, have you found a job yet?" Trying not to get upset about the sarcastic remark Marvin answers, "Not yet Mr. Hawcoms, but I am still looking." "Ok, I warned you, now I'm going to have to give you a time limit. At this time I'm giving you one week to find a job and if you fail to do so, I will bring you before the court, and you will have to explain to the Judge why you are not working or paying on your fines. Do you understand Mr. Anderson?" While Marvin is talking to Mr. Hawcoms, there is a knock at the front door. Louis answers the door, "yo, who you looking for?" "Hello, my name is Stuart Ball and I am looking for a Marvin Anderson." Louis yells Marvin name, "yeah he's here, but he is on an important phone call right now. Would you like to wait for him?" "Sure." Mr. Hawcoms tells Marvin, "I'm not going to put you on a curfew, because eventually you will hang yourself and wind up back in jail anyway. Do you have any questions?" "No sir Mr. Hawcoms." "You have a nice day." "Yes sir Mr. Hawcoms, you do the same."

Marvin hangs up the phone and thinks about calling Leon to make some money so he could pay off his court fines and get Mr. Hawcoms off his back. Then he prays about his thoughts and finding a job. After praying, he walks out into the front room to see what Louis wants. "What's up Louis?" "There is a Stuart Ball at the dining room table looking for you. You know him? He looks like a cop or something." Marvin walked into the dining room, "Hey, I'm Marvin." Stuart stands up and they shake hands as they sit down at the dining room table. 'My name is Stuart Ball, but you can call me Stuart. Let me start by saying I was at your church yesterday. I was invited by a friend, but anyway, I hear that you are an ex-con and an ex-drug dealer. Is that true?" "Yeah, but why are you asking me these questions?"

"Oh I'm sorry, I work for a contractor that works for the state and what we do is help ex-cons make a life after prison. We find jobs, get housing, counseling, basically whatever it takes to start a new life after prison." Marvin's curious, "So you are going to help me find a job?" "Noooo I am here to offer you a job, as an inspirational speaker to ex-cons." "Wait a minute Mr. Ball." "Call me Stuart." "Ok Stuart, are you giving me a job?"

"Yes I am Marvin, are you available to work? Marvin is silent with tears running down his face. "Sorry is this a bad time?" Marvin wiping his face, "No, no, sorry, but these are tears of joy." "Ok, let me explain, we normally don't hire ex-cons. But we would like to make an exception and try someone who has been through what these guys have been through to talk to them and to motivate them. With only a 33 percent progress rate, whatever we are doing now isn't working. I think that the guys would rather hear from someone who they could relate to rather than someone who reads books about their situation. So after seeing you yesterday and hearing about your situation, I convinced my boss to give it a try. And here I am, so… are you available? And if so, would you except $32,000 a year as a start?" Sitting silent Marvin drops his head on the table, face down. Stuart was thinking 32,000 wasn't enough, "well if you can get an associate's degree, you can make 36,000." Stuart doesn't know that Marvin already has his associate's degree. Marvin falls from his chair and gets on his knees, "Thank you Jesus, thank you!" Stuart sees how grateful Marvin is. "Now I must also tell you that this is a one year temporary position that could turn into a full-time position, depending on the percentage numbers. If they go up, then welcome aboard. But if the numbers go down or stay the same, then they will do away with the program." Marvin excited, "Thank you Mr. Ball, I accept your offer. I would love to work for you. Oh by the way, I already have my associate's degree." "Oh good, good, you already got your first raise before day one (laughing). Well if you can come in tomorrow at 8 o'clock and fill out some paper work, we can get started. Here is my card, with my name, number, email and the company's address."

Meanwhile at Kevin's job, Kevin had gone to work early so he could talk to his boss. Walking down the hall to his boss's office, he says a prayer to himself. The door is open so Kevin walks in the office and sees his boss at his desk, "hey Carl you got a minute?" "For you yes sir, have a seat. You and your guys on the night shift are doing a great job." "Well Carl that's what I want to talk to you about, I am going to have to step down as a supervisor." Carl really needs Kevin to stay supervisor at night, so he can keep his job. "Why? What wrong? We really need you to supervise the nightshift." "Everything is ok, it's not the men. It's just that my family needs me and I'm never home. My wife is raising the kids by herself and my oldest boy is getting in trouble and his grades are dropping in school. And I'm missing Church on Sundays." Carl hears Kevin but talking but he doesn't care about Kevin's problems. A few years ago, his family left him because he had put work first, and he doesn't believe in God. "Kevin if that is your only reason, that's not real a problem. I mean your wife needs to step up and take care of the kids and house while you are making money to provide for them." "Carl it's not about having everything, they need me." "Well Kevin we were also talking about giving you a three percent raise." "Carl I prayed on it, and right now my family needs me and I need to get back in church. Money is not important." "Church, did you say church? Wow Kevin, you mean you would rather go to church and give your money to the preacher so he could drive a fancy car and live in a big house. Hey, and when you prayed, did God tell you that you need your job to raise your family?" Carl lies, "Plus your position on the day shift has been filled, so you couldn't go back if I wanted you to." "Well Carl I'm going to do what God called me to do, and He called me to be a father and a husband first. So I guess I have to give you my two week's notice." Carl starts to get angry, "well I'm sorry too Kevin we will miss you, but you have my number. Call me when you come to your senses." Kevin looked at Carl like he was crazy, and didn't say a word. He just stood up and walked out. On the way out of Carl's office Kevin sees Carl's boss, "Hello Mr. Thomas." "Hello there Kevin, how are you?" "I'm ok, I guess. Things will get better".

Kevin kept walking out of the building to his car, and Mr. Thomas walked in Carl's office. "Hey Carl I couldn't help but to hear you all's conversation. Umm, what's going on with Kevin?" "Ahh he's ok, right now he is going through the family and church thing. But he'll realize that his job comes first." "I don't understand what do you mean?" Carl mocking Kevin, "He's claims that he is not spending time with his family and his wife and kids needs him. Oh and he is missing church. You know, all that mumbo jumbo junk, and that he prayed on it and God told him to get his old position back." Carl starts laughing and shaking his head. Mr. Thomas, with his arms folded, grins and walks out of the office.

Meanwhile at Lisa's job, the women in the office had got together and bought Lisa flowers and a card. She was very appreciative and shocked, because she was thinking that the women would be gossiping about what had happened to her Friday. But they are very supportive, and it was all Tanisha's idea. Lisa is sitting at her desk working and feeling happy about the women being supportive, but she is still scared about her situation. Lisa, typing on her computer gets a text message from Rick. "Hey Lisa, what you doing?" Lisa read the message and was surprised to hear from Rick. She is feeling happy, angry, and curious. Holding her phone, she hesitates to answer but she does text back. "Nothing." "I was just thinking about you, missing you and wondering what you were doing." Lisa starts to think about what he had done to her. Answering back angry, "what do you want Rick? Where's your baby mama?" "Deg, I can't text you, just to say hi?" "For what, do you know what you did, look I have to go." "Ok, but I miss you." Lisa slams her phone on the desk and screams. Tanisha came over to her, "Girl, are you ok?" "No I'm not! He had the nerve to text me after what he did." "Lisa he does this stuff because you let him." Lisa is in denial, "what you talking about? I don't let him do nothing." "He knows he has control over you." "Whatcha mean?" Tanisha went over to get her purse and tells Lisa, "Meet me in the break room."

In the break sitting down at a table, Tanisha pulled a Bible out of her purse. "Look Lisa, let me tell you something. Girl you need Jesus, I used to be like you given men all my trust, and they would let me down every time. And then I found myself mad with the world. That's what I mean by giving him power. They were controlling how I felt, how I was acting, even my thoughts. I had no control over myself. But when I met Jesus and put all my trust in Him, I got my power back and He tells me what's good for me. A real man is not going to use and abuse you. I'm going to be honest with you so don't get mad with me, but you kind of brought this on yourself by having sex without protection." Lisa shocked and surprised, "wow Tanisha, I never would have guessed that you read the Bible." "Girl I read all the time, how do you think I make it around here? Let me show you something, you have power and strength." Tanisha opens her Bible, "your strength comes from God, look." Psalm 28:7 The LORD is my strength and my shield; my heart trusts in him, and he helps me. My heart leaps for joy, and with my song I praise him. Psalm 29: 11 The LORD gives strength to his people; the LORD blesses his people with peace. "Lisa you need to be strong, but you can't do it by yourself. You have to come to God and give Him your battles, because He is your strength and your peace." 2 Corinthians 1: 3-4, Praise be to the God and Father of our Lord Jesus Christ, the Father of compassion and the God of all comfort, 4 who comforts us in all our troubles, so that we can comfort those in any trouble with the comfort we ourselves receive from God. "See girl, Jesus is all that and then some! He is the father to your child, why don't you try Him, and leave these no-good men alone. The more you read, the better you will be." Tanisha gets up from the table, "we better get back to work girl." "Thanks Tanisha, I really needed to hear that." Tanisha walks out of the break room, and Lisa is still sitting at the table thinking.

Back at Kevin's house, its dinner time and everyone is sitting at the table. Kevin tells Kim and the kids, "hey y'all I'm quitting my night job and I will be looking for a day job." Jr. is happy to hear that his father will be home, but Kim is curious, "Did you ask for your old day job back?" "Yeah I asked, but Carl said that the position was filled." "Really, so you gave them your two week's notice without another job lined up." "Yes Kim, I prayed about it and I need to be home. I'll find something." "Ok, we better pray together." Before Kevin can answer Kim, the phone rings and Kevin tells Jr. to get it. Jr. runs in the kitchen to answer the phone, "Hello." "Hello, is this the Kevin Jones residence?" "Yeah, who do you want to talk to?" "Mr. Jones." Jr. runs back into the dining room, "dad the phone is for you." Kevin, wiping his hands, gets up from the table and walks into the kitchen to get the phone, "hello this is Kevin." "Hey Kevin, I didn't catch you at a bad time did I?" "No, no I had just finish having dinner, is this Mr. Thomas?" "Yes it is." "Oh ok, is something wrong? "Well Kevin, are you still interested in a day time position?" "Yes sir I am, but Carl said that the position was filled." "Never mind what Carl said, Kevin, I'm going to be straight with you. We have a day time position along with a promotion and weekends off, and the job is yours if you want it." Surprised and confused Kevin answers, "Yes sir, I want the job. What will I be doing?" "Well Kevin, Carl was terminated today, and his position is open. I think that you can handle his position. And don't worry about working tonight, take off the rest of the week and start fresh Monday morning. Carl has to clean out the office." "Thank you Mr. Thomas, thank you I am your man for the job. But what happened to Carl?" "Ahhh let's just say God don't like ugly." "Anyway Thanks again Mr. Thomas." "No Kevin, thank God."

Meanwhile, Robin is at her mother's house. While her mother is cooking, Robin is sitting at the kitchen table trying to figure out a way to tell her mother she needs help with her drug problem. After twenty minutes of talking about everything she blurters out, "mom I have a drug problem and I want some help." Robin's mother looks at her and sees tears rolling down her face. She sees that Robin is serious, so she sits at the table with her. She hugs her and tells her, "Robin it's going to be ok, we are going to get some help from the helper. I am proud of you for recognizing you need help. Your first step is knowing and admitting that you have a problem. Now if you really want to stop, you can, the Lord gave you the power. He is your helper; with Him all things are possible." Robin starts to cry, "But mom I lost everything. I have nothing. I feel like I don't want to live no more." "Robin, God loves you, so you have everything. The devil doesn't want you to know that. He wants you to feel like you lost everything and have nothing to live for. But as long as you know that God loves you, you have everything." Robin still crying, "You don't understand mom, this drug controls me it's like I'm a slave." Robin's mother gets angry and starts talking with force and confidence, "no you don't understand, I been there done that. You don't know but years ago when you was young, I had a drug problem too. I thought I couldn't stop. I'd been in program after program and nothing worked until I met God and I turn it over to the Lord. And I am telling you that your God is more powerful than any strong hold, but you have to believe it. It's time to stop crying and feeling sorry for yourself. It's time to fight back, now go get your Bible." "Go with me to 1 Corinthians 7, it says," [21] Are you a slave? Don't let that worry you—but if you get a chance to be free, take it. [22] And remember, if you were a slave when the Lord called you, you are now free in the Lord. And if you were free when the Lord called you, you are now a slave of Christ. [23] God paid a high price for you, so don't be enslaved by the world. "Now go to John 8." [36] So if the Son sets you free, you are truly free. "Robin if you believe, then you are free, the victory is yours. But you have to pray, read and have faith." Robin and her mother both get on their knees and start to pray together.

Meanwhile at the church,, Pastor Tim is packing his belongings, he is stepping down as Pastor at the church. Taking down pictures off the wall and empting the desk drawers, he hears the church front door open and close. Pastor Tim, still packing, has his back to the office door and hears a knock at the door. "Tim, are you going somewhere?" Pastor Tim turns around, "Tina what are you doing here?" "What, you don't want to see me anymore?" Pastor Tim shakes his head, "No I don't, I was wrong, I let my flesh get the best of me, and this never should have happened. I need to repent and get myself back right with God. Besides, your husband coming here yesterday really open my eyes, it could have been a lot worse." "What? My husband, he was here yesterday?" Tina tries to talk, but Pastor Tim puts his figure over her mouth, "Tina please just leave. Make things right with your husband. I wish I could tell him how sorry I am." Tina's husband John walks in the office, "I heard you, I heard everything." Pastor Tim backs into the corner with his hands up in a surrendering position. Tina shocked and nervous, "John what are you doing here." Hurt and angry, "The question is what are you doing here? I took off of work today to follow you. I had to see it with my own eyes." John shaking his head, "I can't take it no more." John reaches under his shirt and pulls out a gun. Pastor Tim talking fast, "Now John please, don't get yourself in trouble over our stupidity. We made a big mistake and we are very sorry." Tina scared and crying, as John points the gun at her, "I work hard every day to support you and all I get is you cheating on me." Pastor Tim slowly steps between Tina and the gun, "brother please, this does not have to end like this." John shouting, "Brother please, brother please, you are not my brother. You slept with my wife, and I'm going to kill everybody in here." John starts to cry as he cocks back his gun, Pastor Tim closes his eyes and starts praying, then hears a gunshot (POW). Opening his eyes, Pastor Tim sees that John had shot up at the ceiling and dropped the gun crying. Picking the gun up, Pastor Tim hugs John, "brother I am so sorry, but we are going to get through this. God is going to get us through this."

Two days later…

It's Wednesday evening and the church is having a meeting. They are meeting to talk about getting a new Pastor, so tomorrow they are starting to take interviews. Meanwhile at Kevin and Kim's, Kevin is helping Jr. with a school project and Kim is washing dishes. The doorbell rings, Kim shouting, "I got it." "Who is it?" "Detective Pearson." Kim opens the door with a blank look on her face, "Detective Pearson?" "Hello, is you husband and son home?" "Yes, I'll go get them." Kevin comes in the living room upset, "I thought I told you my lawyer will contact you. I don't need detectives hanging around my house." "Hold it before you blow your stack, I came by to tell you that Jr. is in the clear and that Butch was caught trying to steal another car. Then he confessed to the other stolen car after the owner identified him." Kevin and Kim shouting for joy calls Jr. in the room, "It's over son, it's over! Thank You Jesus!"

Meanwhile at grandma's house, Marvin just got in from work. Louis met him in the living room. "Yo, cuz ,how was work today?" "Nice, I'm surrounded by a bunch of women." "Well good because you had a visitor today." "Who?" "Two detectives want to talk to you about that gun that you gave to the security guard at the store." "That was Bobby's gun, what they want to talk to me about?" "They said that the gun was involved in a crime six years ago." Marvin is shocked, "what, I don't know anything about that gun." "Well they said that they would like to ask you some questions, here's his card." After getting the number from Louis, Marvin goes in the kitchen to use the phone, "hello may I speak with a Mr. Milton." "Speaking, how can I help you?" "My name is Marvin Anderson, and you left a number at my house to call you." "Ok yes ummm, I have to ask you a couple of questions about a gun that you gave the security guard at the grocery store." "Hey man that wasn't my gun." "No need to get defensive Mr. Anderson if you have nothing to hide, I just need to ask you a couple of questions." "Yeah I have no problem with that, when is a good time to talk." "I tell you what, my partner and I can be there in a half hour." "I'll be here."

Marvin hangs up the phone and hopes that nothing is wrong. He went to his room to change his clothes. A half hour is up and Marvin walks to the front door, he sees no one so he sits on the couch. Two minutes later the doorbell rings. Marvin jumps up and opens the door, "Mr. Milton." "Yes sir, are you Marvin?" "Yeah come on in." Marvin escorting them to the dining room table, "Marvin just call me Jeff, and this is my partner Tom." "Alright." Everybody's sitting at the table. Tom has a pen and pad while Jeff is asking the questions. "Well Marvin, how are you making out since you been home?" "I'm maintaining, how did you know that I was gone away?" "We looked up your background, it's part of the procedure when an investigation is involved." "Investigation?" "Investigation, about what?" "We're just trying to find out some information about that gun you found. You did find that gun right?" "Man look, I don't know what is going on, or what you are trying to say, but that gun was not mine." Jeff laughing, "I didn't say that I asked you did you find it, but anyway was Chucky Lucas a friend of yours?" Marvin feeling surprised and shocked, "yeah I knew Chucky. Why?" "Well Marvin the gun that you gave to the security guard was used to murder Mr. Chucky Lucas six years ago." There is silence and Marvin is thinking that Bobby must have robbed and killed Chucky. "Wow I don't know what to say." "Well it would help if you have any information that you could share with us." Marvin shaking his head, "Sorry, I know nothing." "I hope you are being honest with us, because as of now you are the only link between

172

Chucky and that gun that killed him." Marvin puts his hands up, "ok I think that it is time to go. I have nothing else to say."

Meanwhile at a pool hall in DC, a couple of teens name Joe and Chris are there playing pool. This is a hangout spot. Some come to play pool, talk junk, and others come to sell drugs. While playing pool, Joe leans over the table to make a shot and started talking about what had happened to Butch, "Yo, I heard that Butch got locked up." "Yeah that's my homie, I heard that this youngin name Kevin snitched him out." "For real, that's not good." "Na, youngin gonna pay, he won't tell on nobody else." "I'll make sure to warn everybody about this dude." Now the rumor that Jr. had told on Butch just started. It's Sunday morning and everybody is at church this morning to hear a word from God through their temporary Pastor. Grandma sat beside Marvin and asked him, "Have you seen the Pastor yet." "No." Marvin shaking his head up and down, "but I heard that he is a good teacher and a preacher, and that he wouldn't accept money to preach." "Really? I'll be right back, Kevin asked me to get Jr., he's out front." Robin is up front singing with the choir and the Deacon walked out onto the pulpit to introduce the temporary Pastor. "After the choir sings, the next voice you will hear will be Pastor James Trolley. Marvin with a strange look on his face tells grandma, "That name sounds familiar.""

After the choir stopped singing, out came Pastor James Trolley walking out onto the pulpit, but Marvin doesn't recognize him at first. Then Pastor Trolley says, "good morning church, I believe that God sent me here to save souls by giving you his instruction on life." Marvin recognizes those words and looks at him again, talking low to himself, "hey that's Rev." Rev talking to everybody, "turn your Bible to Romans 7:21, it says." [21] I have discovered this principle of life— that when I want to do what is right, I inevitably do what is wrong. [22] I love God's law with all my heart. [23] But there is another power within me that is at war with my mind. This power makes me a slave to the sin that is still within me. [24] Oh, what a miserable person I am! Who will free me from this life that is dominated by sin and death? [25] Thank God! The answer is in Jesus Christ our Lord, "Now turn your bible to Luke 5:31. It says, "Jesus answered them, Healthy people don't need a doctor—sick people do. [32] I have come to call not those who think they are righteous, but those who know they are sinners and need to repent."

After reading the scriptures, Jr. came running into the church, "somebody help please, somebody help, grandma's been shot!"

Made in the USA
Columbia, SC
27 February 2022

56919237R00107